THE
·DOORMAN·

OTHER BOOKS BY REINALDO ARENAS

THE
· DOORMAN ·

Reinaldo Arenas

Translated from the Spanish
by Dolores M. Koch

GROVE PRESS

NEW YORK

Published simultaneously in Canada
Printed in the United States of America

Library of Congress Cataloging-in-Publication Data

Arenas, Reinaldo, 1943–
    [Portero. English]
    The doorman / Reinaldo Arenas ; translated from the Spanish
by Dolores M. Koch.
        p. cm.
    Translation of: El portero.
    1. Cubans—New York (N.Y.)—Fiction. 2. Refugees,
Political—New York (N.Y.)—Fiction. 3. Refugees, Political—
Cuba—Fiction. 4. Apartment houses—New York (N.Y.)—
Fiction. I. Title.
PQ7390.A72P613
863—dc20   90-28775
ISBN-13: 978-0-8021-3405-9

Design by Joyce C. Weston

Grove Press
an imprint of Grove/Atlantic, Inc.
841 Broadway
New York, NY 10003

Distributed by Publishers Group West

www.groveatlantic.com

13 14 15 16 17 18   10 9 8 7 6 5

For Lázaro, his novel

It was the true light
that enlightens every man
who comes into the world.

John 1:9

·PART ONE·

· PART ONE ·

· 1 ·

THIS is the story of Juan, a young man who was dying of grief. We can't explain the exact causes of that grief, and much less what it was like. For if we could, then his heartache would not have been so terrible and this story would make no sense, since nothing extraordinary would have happened to him and we would not have taken so much interest in his case.

Sometimes his whole face would cloud over, as if the intensity of his sadness had reached a climax. But then, as if the suffering had abated, his features would soften, giving the sadness an appearance of peaceful serenity: the disenchantment was perhaps resting now, somehow aware that its immense power would never be exhausted, but on the contrary would keep growing and regenerating itself forever.

Ten years ago Juan had fled his native Cuba in a boat, and settled in the United States. He was seventeen then, and his entire past life had been left behind: humiliations and warm beaches, fierce enemies and loving friends whom the very persecutions had made even more special. Left behind was slavery, but the complicity of the night as well, and cities made to the measure of his restlessness; unbounded horror, but also a human quality, a state of mind, a sense of brotherhood in the face of terror — all things that, just like his own way of being, were alien here. . . . But we, too (and there are a million of us), left all that behind; and yet, we are not dying of grief (at least no one has seen us dying) so hopelessly as this young man. Still, as we already said, we can't pretend to be able to explain his case; instead, so far as possible, we can only tell what happened. And even then, to say it in a language we haven't really mastered, while at the same time forgetting our native tongue, which, like so many other things and for obvious reasons, we have had to forget.

We don't mean to boast that we gave this young man any special treatment. None was called for. He arrived in the United States as an unskilled laborer, like most of us, just one more person escaping from Cuba. He needed to learn, just as we did, the value of things, the high price one must pay for a stable life: a well-paying job, an apartment, a car, vacations, and finally one's own house, preferably near the ocean. . . . Because the sea is our natural element. And it has to be the real ocean, an ocean that we can dive into and feel comfortable, not like the icy, gray expanses over here, where we have to cover ourselves almost from head to foot. . . .

Yes, we know these confessions are overly sentimental, thoughts that our powerful community, we ourselves, would totally deny or brand as unnecessary and ridiculous. We are practical, respectable citizens, many of us quite wealthy, and part of a nation that is still the most powerful in the world. But the subject of our testimony is an exceptional case. It is the story of a young man who, unlike us, could not or would not adjust to this practical world. On the contrary: he explored absurd and desperate paths, and worse yet, paths where he attempted to take with him everyone he met. Idle gossips, of which there are never too few, say that he upset animals as well, but we will talk about that later. . . . We can already anticipate the objections from the reporters, professors, and critics who are waiting to pounce on us. If this is *Juan's story*, they'll say, there's no reason for our constant interruptions to interpose *our own* concerns. Once and for all, let's make it clear, first, that we don't (fortunately) belong to a writers' union, and therefore don't have to obey its rules; second, that our young man, as part of our community, is also a part of ourselves; and third, that we were the ones who opened the doors of this new world for him, and who were always ready "to lend a helping hand," as we used to say over there, in the place that we fled.

As soon as he arrived — and in very bad shape — we helped him financially (with more than two hundred dollars), we assisted him in obtaining a Social Security card, so that he could pay his taxes, and almost immediately, we also got him a job. Obviously it couldn't be a job like the ones we now have, after twenty or thirty years of hard work in this country. We got him a job in construction — naturally, out in the sun. It seems that Juan then started to get terrible headaches from exposure. All of a sudden he would stop in the middle of work, a bucket of cement mix in each hand, and he would just stand there, staring into space, as though dazzled by some mysterious revelation. Just imagine, amid the feverish construction work, this young man standing there completely paralyzed, shirtless, a bucket in each hand, and babbling through the din of sledge-hammers and buzz saws. . . . The foreman, in a rage, would yell in English (which Juan still did not understand) all sorts of orders and insults. But only after that moment of illumination or madness was over would Juan return to his job.

Of course, we had to find him job after job. He worked as a waiter in a bar in Southwest Miami (La Sauecera), cleaning bathrooms at a hospital for Haitian refugees, as a presser in a mid-Manhattan garment factory, as a ticket-seller at a 42nd Street movie house. . . . And what did you expect? Should we have offered him our swimming pools? Or, just because of his pretty face (he wasn't ugly; none of us is, with our natural tan, not like these flabby, pale, ill-proportioned figures so common here), yes, for his pretty face were we supposed to have invited him into our mansions in Coral Gables? Or to have handed him the keys to our latest-model cars so he could win the love of our daughters, whom we have raised with so much loving care? In short, should we have let him enjoy the good life without first having learned the price one has to pay in this world for every breath of air? Not for a minute!

Finally, when we saw that he was unfit for any job that would require character, initiative, and "spark," or *chispa*, as we used to say in our old world, we managed to find him work (and it wasn't easy, in a line controlled by the Mafia) on the staff of an apartment building in the most luxurious residential section of Manhattan. His job could not have been simpler or less stressful: all he had to do was open the door and respectfully greet the residents of the building. *Doorman* — that was his new career.

But if we had problems with Juan concerning all of his previous jobs, we must state that with this one our real headaches began. Not precisely because Juan neglected his duties; rather because he was *overzealous*. For suddenly our doorman discovered (or thought he had discovered) that his tasks could not be limited to just opening the door of the building — but that he, the doorman, was the one *chosen, elected, singled out* (take your pick) from all mankind to show everyone who lived there a wider door, until then either invisible or inaccessible: the door to their own lives, which Juan described as — and we must quote him exactly even though it may seem (and, in fact, be) ridiculous — "the door to true happiness."

Of course, not even Juan himself knew what this door was or how to find it, much less how to open it. But in his state of exaltation, or delirium or dementia (take your pick again), he was sure this door really existed, and in some mysterious way one might reach and open it.

He thought, and left testimony to that effect in the countless pages of notes he scribbled while being a doorman, that homes or apartments transcended the limits of their outer walls, that the lives of the people who lived in the building where he was the doorman could not be confined to the eternal shuffling from kitchen to bathroom, from living room to bedroom, or from elevator to car. It was utterly inconceivable to him that these people's existence — and, by extension, everybody's — was nothing but a coming and going from one cubicle into another, from one small space into an even smaller one, from office to bedroom, from train to coffee shop, from subway to bus, and so on, forever and ever, forever and ever. . . . He would show them "other places," for he would not only open the glass door for them, but would (and we quote again) "lead them into dimensions never before suspected, into timeless regions with no material limits." . . . Deep in these thoughts, he would pace the lobby of the building from one end to the other, talking to himself incoherently, though always, we must admit, attentive to the door, in his impeccable uniform (blue jacket and pants, elegant black cap, white gloves, and golden epaulets). So whenever he felt unobserved, after checking every corner with apprehension, he would walk to the lobby and face his own reflection in the great mirror, or would stop at the broad door leading to the inner courtyard, where he would then surreptitiously scribble something in the little notebook he always carried. At other times, he would stroll through the courtyard, gloved hands clasped behind his back, wondering how he could show all those people the path (which, of course, was also unknown to him). And suddenly he would abandon his meditations and rush to open the big glass door for various tenants, and perhaps carry their packages to their apartments while inquiring about their health and even about the health of their dog, their cat, their parrot, their monkey, or their fish. . . . Please don't forget that in this country you are supposed to have either a dog, a canary, a cat, or some other animal (no matter what kind). Aberrations, we agree, morbid pastimes for idle or lonely people who have no other means of entertainment. Typical habits, after all, of batty old women — and men no less loony — who, most of the time, seem like decent and normal people.

Now we understand that there was method in Juan's small favors. For his *work*, let us call it that, consisted of being extremely gracious to all the tenants in the building, in the hope of winning their friendship, gaining access to their apartments, and then to their lives, which he intended to change.

Let us now introduce quickly and concisely (for we are all very busy and cannot spend the rest of our lives on this) the tenants with whom our doorman somehow managed to relate. These are the most outstanding: Mr. Roy Friedman, a gentleman some sixty-five years old — the "candy man" in Juan's diary, because he always had one in his mouth and more in his pockets, and every time he met the doorman, which was naturally several times a day, he gave him a piece of candy.

Dr. Joseph Rozeman, a famous dental engineer, thanks to whom many of the most beautiful television and movie stars display glamorous smiles. (Notable members of our own community have also used Dr. Rozeman's services, and we assure you that they are highly recommended.)

Next on our list is Mr. John Lockpez, an Ecuadorian who is now a U.S. citizen and a pastor of the Church of Love of Christ Through Friendly and Constant Contact. He is married with children, and they are all, including his wife, very religious. Mr. Lockpez, originally Juan López, took a quick liking to our doorman and tried to win him over to his cause (Mr. Lockpez's, of course), thus establishing, we can testify, a fanatical contest between the two men, with each trying to convert the other to his own peculiar doctrine. Anyway, we will give you more details later about these relationships. This is only a list.

Let us proceed, then, with Miss (or Mrs.) Brenda Hill, a rather free woman, single, and slightly alcoholic; Mr. Arthur Makadam, an older gentleman though still a libertine; Miss Mary Avilés, who was supposedly the doorman's fiancée; Mr. Stephen Warrem, the building's millionaire-in-residence, who lives with his family in the penthouse; Mrs. Cassandra Levinson, officially a "Professor of Social Sciences," and an indefatigable champion of Fidel Castro; Mr. Pietri, the building super, and his family; Messrs. Oscar Times (or Oscar Times One and Oscar Times Two), a homosexual pair who resemble each other so closely, both in body and in temperament, that they really appear to be the same person — so much so that many tenants who have never seen them together think there is only one of them. But we know there are two, and even that one of them is Cuban. . . . Miss Scarlett Reynolds, a retired actress obsessed with the need to save money, and who also had several conversations with the doorman, as did Professor Walter Skirius, a noted scientist and inveterate inventor.

With all these people our doorman managed — through friendliness, flattery, and little favors above and beyond the call of duty — to somehow relate or at least achieve a degree of rapport, however patronizing on their part; and sometimes he was able to be not only their doorman, but also their guest. This accomplishment showed (or so Juan thought) that he had made great strides on his missionary path.

WHEN Mr. Roy Friedman invited the doorman to his apartment for the first time, Juan thought his mission was well under way. Now he only needed to convince Mr. Friedman to join him in the quest for that true door. But Mr. Friedman had his own philosophy too, his secret door through which he wanted to push anyone who came close enough to him. Like all self-assured people, Mr. Friedman did not listen, he just talked: he would not take advice, he would give it.

"How long do you think I have been living in this building?" he asked the doorman, after inviting him to sit down and giving him a piece of candy. Juan was going to make a wild guess — ten, twenty years. But Mr. Friedman did not allow Juan even to begin formulating a response and proudly proclaimed: "Twenty-eight years, three months, and six days! And yet, you are the first doorman I have ever invited into my home. . . ."

Juan was ready to thank him for such an exceptional honor when a huge dog came into the living room and began to sniff the doorman with apparent disgust.

"Come here, Vigilante," Mr. Friedman commanded the gigantic dog, and taking out of his pocket a bone-shaped piece of candy, offered it to the dog. The animal took it reluctantly but dutifully, and went off to chew it in a corner. While doing this he glanced at the doorman, who thought he saw a kind of resigned sadness in those eyes.

"Your dog is so well trained," commented Juan, watching the poor animal trying to swallow the gooey candy.

"Yes," continued Mr. Friedman, without having listened to Juan's words, "you are the first doorman to enter my home. Something exceptional. And it is all because I believe I see in you certain talents, a certain touch of originality, and also a touch of restlessness. Since you began working here, more than seven months ago — "

Nine, Juan was going to say, but Mr. Friedman did not stop talking: "Yes, in these seven months I never had to write a letter of complaint to the building management. You have never left your post, never failed to open the door properly for me."

"The door, that's the most important thing," Juan managed to squeeze in, with great effort.

"Of course that is most important, that is the reason for your being our doorman. But there is something else, which for me is much more significant: you have always accepted my pieces of candy with appreciation. For some people, well, for nearly everyone, this would seem a superfluous detail. And yet, do you know what is the real basis for achieving success in life?" At this point Mr. Friedman glanced questioningly at Juan, who thought this was the right moment to slip in a word about the reason for his appreciativeness.

"Well, the key to success is giving and receiving sweets, yes, candy!" Mr. Friedman declared categorically. "Whoever is not prepared to offer candy is not prepared to be on good terms with the human race. And oh, above all, he who does not accept it is totally lost!"

Juan nodded and even thought of showing him his jacket pocket filled with the candies Mr. Friedman had given him that week, but changed his mind fearing that his host might feel offended to find out that he had not eaten them.

Mr. Friedman had not stopped talking.

"I have noticed how you are always reading, and even writing, whenever your work does not claim your attention, and that is very commendable. But the *answer*, my friend, is not to be found in reading books or in writing. Where do you think the problem lies, and where the solution?"

Then Mr. Friedman stood in silence in the center of the living room, looked around with an air of mystery, and after reaching into his pants pocket, handed the doorman a piece of candy.

"The problem and its solution lie in human relationships; naturally, such relationships should be developed in a simple, practical, and effective manner. A piece of candy today, another one tomorrow. In this way, day in and day out, the spirit of generosity that we all have inside (buried very deep sometimes) will spring forth and blossom. And the day will come, let me assure you, my friend, when we will all be giving and receiving candy. From that moment on, when the whole world, arms extended, is either giving or receiving, then true brotherhood for all mankind will begin and with it, naturally, total happiness."

Again Mr. Friedman turned around in the room and walked toward Vigilante to give him another caramel-filled bone, which the dog, looking so contrite, took between his teeth and let out a short, involuntary whimper.

"I think," Juan ventured quickly, "that a piece of candy is not enough. I think we have to look for — "

"More! Of course we have to look for more, we have to give more! Of course a piece of candy is not enough. I know that very well. You are very smart. Smarter than I had imagined. Now I am going to show you the secret of my success with the human race. But first, tell me: have you ever seen me argue with any of the tenants? Have I had even the slightest disagreement with the super — who, between you and me, is very obnoxious. Have I had the slightest disagreement or unkind word with Brenda Hill or with Mrs. Levinson? And the same applies to everyone I have dealt with over the course of my long life. Why has it been that way? For this simple reason."

And taking the doorman by the arm, Roy Friedman led him to the most important room in his apartment.

The two men were now in a room full of shelves and cabinets

that reached all the way to the ceiling. And all of the compartments, drawers, cabinets, and boxes were filled to overflowing with candy of every color, flavor, shape, and size imaginable. Suddenly Mr. Friedman began opening doors, emptying drawers and boxes, and scattering thousands of pieces of candy everywhere. Onto the carpeted floor spilled candies in the shape of mythological animals, of women, children, birds, fish, saints, and of completely unknown objects and animals. Our doorman tried to stop Mr. Friedman, telling him that it was all right, that he was absolutely convinced of his labor of love. But Mr. Friedman, as if possessed and no longer aware of the doorman's presence, had clambered up a stepladder and was emptying huge cartons from the top shelves, from which brightly wrapped toffees of all sizes were cascading. Juan tried to speak to him again, but Mr. Friedman, awash in the riches of that outlandish rain, was still babbling in ecstasy.

Seeing that for now it would be impossible to sustain any kind of dialogue with that man, Juan respectfully took his leave, though without being heard. Back in the living room, he bowed ceremoniously and moved toward the hallway. As he was leaving, his eyes met those of the gigantic dog, and it seemed to the doorman that the animal, while still chewing his taffylike candy, gave him a look that combined both pity and mockery.

· 3 ·

WE have decided, after prolonged discussions, that Juan should not have abandoned Mr. Friedman under those circumstances, and that his duty as doorman and guest was to have helped him put all those pieces of candy back in their respective containers. But, of course, it is also true that duty demanded he return to his post at the entrance of the building. In any case, we are recording here the events as they happened, not as we wish they had. On the other hand — and this is extremely important for the reader to understand from the very beginning — the fact that we are a million people signing this document compels us to try to reach a middle ground in our opinions or, using an expression popular in this land, *to present a balanced picture*. We recognize that many of us at times would prefer to be harsher with some of the characters in this presentation, while being more lenient with others, and even to leave out completely the unscrupulous acts of a few who are truly immoral. But the general consensus among our signers was rather not to interfere with the objectivity of the present testimony, which, as you shall see, is our most powerful weapon. . . . Having made this clear, we feel obliged to go on with our story.

BACK at his post, Juan let in and warmly greeted Mr. Arthur Makadam, a retired attorney who, despite being sixty-seven, still fancied himself a real Don Juan. He arrived, in fact, accompanied by a typical American beauty (tall, blond, healthy, and strong but, we must recognize in honor of truth, with ankles too thick and no hip curves, unlike our own women).... Mr. Makadam, with the air of an oil magnate, took out a $100 bill from his leather wallet and waved it before handing it to the doorman, who bowed ceremoniously but without harboring any illusions. He knew (for this had already happened several times) that when his lady guest had departed, Arthur Makadam would demand his bill back, handing him a quarter in exchange.

Mr. Makadam's intentions were quite obvious: with his apparently generous tips he meant to impress his lady friend of the day, and there were many of them.... But Mr. Makadam — whether in giving or taking his bill — always had for the doorman a wink of complicity, and Juan always fondly appreciated this token of roguish camaraderie or silent agreement. That old man with his womanizing delusions, our doorman thought, was a lonely soul and therefore in need of some guidance, a way out (or in) to another place; toward that mysterious door, which of course he, Juan, was going to open for him.

A few minutes after Mr. Makadam's return, Juan opened the door for Brenda Hill. This lady, always a bit tipsy, walked in serenely, greeting the doorman with an impersonal "Hi," and then, head high in aristocratic style, she took the elevator. But as soon as she reached her apartment, she called Juan on the intercom. With her ladylike authority, she requested his presence at her apartment, claiming there was something wrong with her telephone.

This kind of predicament — tenants with an overflowing toilet, a telephone out of order, a burned-out light bulb, or collapsed windowshades — occurred almost every day. And even though neither the doorman's duties nor his skills had anything to do with these tasks, Juan, on behalf of his other mission, was eager to oblige whenever called upon.

When he reached her apartment, Brenda Hill was waiting for him wrapped in a long, yellow dressing gown. It seemed that the telephone had started working again all by itself, because Mrs. Hill was holding the receiver and carrying on a lively conversation. Without interrupting her chat, she beckoned the doorman to sit on the sofa, where a cat, also yellow, glared at him, bristling and arching her back. Brenda Hill continued her telephone conversation for thirty-five minutes. After hanging up, she went to the refrigerator, mixed a bottle of vodka with orange juice, filled two glasses, and offered one to Juan before sitting next to him on the sofa. She pushed away the cat, who was infuriated.

Juan was about to thank Brenda Hill when he thought this might be a good occasion to engage in a deep discussion with the elegant lady (or so the doorman thought), for, if she was always drinking or having male visitors or making phone calls, it must be because she was searching for something, *something* she still needed to find: the famous door that he would one day discover.

But Mrs. Brenda Hill, without a word, tossed down her screwdriver and the doorman's as well, and proceeded, with delicate touch and professional skill, to undress him.

She did this so fast that even we (who see everything, don't forget) were amazed.

What was our doorman supposed to do? Stand up, pull up his pants, excuse himself, and disappear? His profession and his status as an employee of the building in fact made him Mrs. Hill's underling, and therefore placed him in an extreme moral dilemma that also jeopardized his job. On the one hand, wasn't it lacking in respect to bed down with Mrs. Hill? And on the other, not to do it and leave — couldn't that be seen as an act of contempt and even of insubordination? In that case, couldn't the spurned Mrs. Hill register a complaint against him with the management for almost anything? . . .

Juan looked up and his eyes met the angry yellow eyes of the cat — was she a Persian? an Abyssinian? a Hindu? (well, we are no cat specialists). And the expression of hatred in that look somehow seemed to tell him, or warn him, that it would be better to allow Mrs. Hill to caress him, even though the same cat, with her arched back, seemed disgusted with the whole scene. It is also true, we won't deny it, that our young doorman felt a certain pleasure at Mrs. Hill's expert handling, as she freed herself from her gown and possessed him, uttering such sharp cries of pleasure that even the cat howled and leapt to the balcony.

After the coupling, Mrs. Hill covered herself again with the gown, buttoning it up to her neck. Then, with a gesture of her well-manicured hand, she dismissed Juan.

"Whenever you're in the mood, give me a ring."

The doorman straightened his uniform and left. Out in the hallway, he realized his break had ended and he had to return to his post by the big glass door.

POISED in the sky, the plump, silvery body of the Goodyear blimp floated up and down like a gigantic fish sniffing cautiously at the skyscrapers; farther off, a small squadron of helicopters kept their blades in motion like hydras swimming to lower depths; and closer, a multicolored balloon with dangling cables ascended like a giant jellyfish, while way up high the fat-bellied jets glided back and forth, much like sharks' undersides seen by someone leagues below. At this time of day when the sky was so intensely blue that the skyline seemed to melt, shrouded in an even darker blue, New York became in the doorman's eyes an immense, underwater city. And the people, who had started to leave the factories, stores, and offices, rushing in all directions, disappearing through subway openings — didn't they look exactly like a school of small fish seeking temporary refuge? From behind the big glass door, that is how our doorman saw the world as he waited for the New York night to fall. But twilight, unaccompanied by shadows, was on the contrary a luminous explosion: a burst of sparks that invaded the skies and even seemed to splash all over the clouds. The twin towers of the World Trade Center were already a faded yellow while the Empire State Building turned an even more desolate hue. And all the other buildings, silhouetted like high sierras against the sky, with their cagelike windows all aglow and twinkling, were sending the doorman their urgent message.

Then a unanimous roar came from the whole city, as if the

disparate and unidentifiable noises produced in that universe by the powers of night had suddenly converged into a single loud howl. And it was a clamoring for Juan (at least that is how our doorman perceived it and recorded it in writing). It was in moments like these that Juan's forebodings — his premonitions, his madness — intensified: that he was without a doubt the one destined to spread throughout the world some kind of message, a new reality, something true and unique, concrete and elusive; a consolation, a solution, a generalized happiness that would be at the same time very personal. A unique and ever-changing door that would offer salvation to each and every person, one by one. But *what was it, what was it, what was it?* . . . A sort of hysterical euphoria would come over him; and then, possessed by his inexplicable delusion of "unknown" powers, by an outlandish belief or absurd visitation, he would mumble to himself, faster and faster, and feel compelled to scribble impassioned, cryptic entries in the notebook he always carried under his uniform, while little cries of joy interrupted his incoherent words: *you are the light, the one who keeps the vigil, the one destined to open all the tunnels, and bring forth the truth that will make possible* . . . All of this and more he wrote in his diary, amid choked moans and apprehensive glances to every corner. And he would start pacing in circles around the lobby, which, bathed in the incandescent luxury of chandeliers, became a miniature replica of the world outside. Next to an outsized, waterless fish tank, our doorman in full blue uniform, high cap, white gloves, golden buttons and braid, also seemed like an exotic fish desperately lunging against the glass, looking for a way out that did not exist, already feeling the lack of oxygen that would soon condemn him to die.

While in this peculiar state of anxiety, he felt a hand pressing his shoulder.

"*Luz y amor,*" said a voice in Spanish, with an American accent.

Quickly turning around, the doorman bumped into the well-groomed figure of Mr. John Lockpez.

"Radiance and love! Light and love, and spiritual growth!" repeated Mr. Lockpez, becoming more enthusiastic and shaking hands vigorously with the doorman.

Once he had squeezed the doorman's hands for five minutes, he held his wrists, his arms, squeezed his shoulders, and patted him repeatedly on the back. Next, he tapped him several times on the forehead and on the stomach, while at the same time crossing himself. Later, with the tips of his fingers, Mr. Lockpez touched Juan's nose and, finally, gently tugged at his ears.

"Radiance and spiritual growth!" he said once more. Again he crossed himself and, with his arms held high, began whirling around the doorman.

Before assigning to these gestures and manipulations any evil intent on the part of Mr. López — sorry, Mr. Lockpez — we should clarify his motives. As representative and Supreme Pastor in New York and for all of the Union of the Church of Love of Christ Through Friendly and Constant Contact, Mr. Lockpez had a special theory. His theory (and he always practiced what he preached) consisted of "promoting the happiness of the human race through brotherly contact." According to him all human beings, and even animals and things, emit some sort of positive radiation "both communicative and receptive," which if not utilized would be wasted, scattering into the air and causing great universal frustration. This *radiation* is a sort of "amorous effluvium" that must be sent out and received "to live in the grace of the Lord and, therefore, in perpetual peace and happiness." For that reason and in accordance with his faith, Mr. Lockpez does not overlook any living creature or inanimate object. Everything that comes his way is touched, felt, passionately if surreptitiously, by the pastor. We hasten to say, since we have been able to confirm this, that these contacts, though physical, have an eminently spiritual source. At no time, and this we assert categorically for we have investigated it in depth, has Mr. Lockpez's high level of physical communication with his fellow beings been obscene in nature. He and all his followers sincerely believe that only through this constant contact with others can the human race find salvation. That is Mr. Lockpez's incessant preaching to our doorman, as well as to any other being or thing in the building. Precisely now, again repeating his catechism, Mr. Lockpez is fingering the armchairs, the lamps, the frame of the big glass door, the desk with the intercom panel, the artificial flowers, and even the tail of Brenda Hill's cat, who has just been taken out for a walk in her owner's arms.

Obviously, this innocent preaching (and its practice) has generated countless problems for Mr. Lockpez, such as being accused of "public lasciviousness" (we have copies of the testimony). These very charges forced him to abandon his native country together with many of his disciples; even fleeing persecution through the rain forest, never for a moment did they break the human chain of contact, at least through the tips of their fingers. According to Mr. Lockpez, only this constant communion with one another's positive radiations could have given his pilgrims enough energy to cross all of Central America on foot, to go through the Panama Canal underwater, to traverse the Mexican deserts, forever teeming with bandits, and finally to swim (but always touching a neighbor, elbow to elbow, toe to toe, or even hair to hair) across the border into the United States.

Mr. Lockpez now has his Church of Love of Christ Through Friendly and Constant Contact in uptown Manhattan, where hundreds of followers meet. His own apartment is also a center for his physico-spiritual sessions. That same evening there was to be a session at his home for a select group of followers, and Mr. Lockpez was urging our doorman to attend.

"I have been observing you for months," he said, touching Juan's forehead with his index finger, "and I think you belong with us. I am never wrong in these matters. I see in you a great need of communication, which our tacto-spiritual circle can fulfill for you."

Juan excused himself by saying that he would not get off from his post as doorman until midnight.

"Exactly when our program will be starting!" countered Mr. Lockpez, tapping Juan's chin. "That is the time when the vibrations are most powerful and you can capture them at their peak. We'll be waiting for you," he added, squeezing Juan's shoulders and giving him a parting slap on his neck.

Juan was about to say it would be impossible for him to attend, that his exhaustion at that hour would prevent him from capturing radiations of any kind. But Mr. Lockpez gave him a military salute and, placing an open palm over Juan's head, cried, "We are expecting you!" He turned around quickly and, caressing the wall on his way, disappeared into the elevator.

• 5 •

AFTER being on his feet for eight hours at the main entrance of the building, bowing and smiling, carrying packages, answering the telephone and the intercom, stepping out to open and close car doors, and praising the intelligence of the tenants' pets, Juan still had to take a train clear across Manhattan to his room on the West Side before he could relax and go to sleep. Could he really slight and perhaps offend Mr. Lockpez, who had always been so kind to him? And on the other hand, wasn't this the perfect opportunity to establish a relationship with this man, with his family and friends? Instead of being the one proselytized, he, the doorman, could attempt to win them over to his own cause, the search for that transcendent, if essentially imprecise, door. With this idea in mind, Juan left his uniform in the closet assigned to the building's doormen and, dressed in a dark suit, went up to Mr. Lockpez's apartment.

"Welcome to this temple, which is your house as well as mine!" was Mr. Lockpez's greeting while he held both of Juan's hands. Then, patting him on the neck and pulling at his ears gently, he began introducing the members of his family. His wife's greeting was to touch his cheeks with two of her fingers; their older boys and girls danced around Juan touching his head; the younger ones, hampered by their height, could only reach up to his knees, which they kept knocking as if his legs were made of wood and they needed to find out how solid they were. Even though the other members of his congregation had not arrived yet, Mr. Lockpez had begun to preach his general sermon, which ran more or less like this:

"By means of spontaneous and affectionate contact that is truly without ulterior motives, radiant love springs forth and spreads. This inexhaustible molecular warmth is a permanent source of joy, human and divine, because through this incessant contact we exchange pure emissions with superior elements. Anguish, loneliness, sorrow, and desperation cannot thrive in our spirit if we are in constant communion with another positive spirit, and each with the next until, like the peaks in an immense mountain range, they form an infinite chain of beneficent energy that combats the Evil One."

While Mr. Lockpez got more and more involved in his passionate sermon, always somehow touching both his relatives and the doorman, all the faithful were coming in, each linking with him and the others, and soon everybody was touching and being touched. Our doorman, in between one touch and the next, which (it must be said) never involved erogenous zones, managed to glance around Mr. Lockpez's living room. In one corner was a birdcage where two small doves tied to each other by their wings fluttered about, helplessly united. Farther on, two golden fish in an aquarium, strung together by their gills, swam round and round. Inside a huge bottle swarmed some flies apparently coupled by a remarkable glue. Next to them, in a larger container, several lizards and other small reptiles crept about, also all tied in pairs. On a ring suspended from the ceiling two parrots joined at the wings, just like the doves, promenaded endlessly in the unbearable din of their patter. Some pigeons, also linked in pairs, flapped their wings near the ceiling, together with other birds that our doorman couldn't identify immediately. Juan noticed that the many cats and dogs going back and forth were also bound, and even a couple of turtles struggled ahead very slowly with their shells connected. There were cockroaches and mice in abundance, all in twos like Siamese twins. Even the ornamental plants on the windows of the apartment were strung together leaf to leaf, forming an impenetrable jungle in miniature. And through that jungle two rats scurried about, apparently tied too. . . . Evidently in that household the philosophy of physical contact, as an inexhaustible source of love and peace, encompassed every living being.

Let us say that this philosophy (we don't know how else to call it) has caused Mr. Lockpez a lot of trouble, in his own country as well as in New York. His harmless but fervent fanaticism sometimes compels him to touch people on trains, at the movies, or out in the street, and this has brought upon him, and will continue to bring, all sorts of insults, arrests, and fines (ranging, up to now, between $25 and $2,000). But Mr. Lockpez and his followers consider these hardships as *trials* of their faith that they should face with integrity, to emerge strengthened and even more unified. During one such legal proceeding, John Lockpez managed to touch the judge's nose, which meant a new charge and trial for *contempt of court*, and a $1,000 cash fine. At the hearing for this incident Mr. Lockpez simply declared that he "recognized the risks of his mission as well as the magnitude of its importance."

By the wee hours of the morning the religious fervor of the congregation fostered by Mr. Lockpez reached a feverish pitch. The apartment was overcrowded with people of all races and ages, whirling about and touching one another at the same time. Finally the rhythm of the Constant Contact followers accelerated while they all were humming a sort of hymn, between a moan and a murmur, reminiscent of a lullaby. They were all rocking from side to side and caressing one another as if soothing themselves to sleep. Three hours went by and the ceremony, instead of ending, grew in intensity. Their heads, fingertips, the palms of their hands, their shoulders, the soles of their feet, their knees were all touching; and even their fingernails, necks, and tips of their hair. And during this ritual our doorman was pushed, shoved, trapped; since he had had nothing to eat and was exhausted after a whole day of intense work, he felt about to faint. . . . Suddenly, the parrots, doves, and other caged birds were set free into the room, together with the rest of the imprisoned animals. And the place became like a chaotic

Noah's Ark, where a dog was compelled to lick a lizard, and a cat had to kiss, or at least nuzzle, a parrot with affection. Meanwhile, above their heads, birds tied by the feet or feathers would screech, trill, or chirp while the faithful, arms held high, tried to reach and caress them. Taking advantage of this confusion, and pretending to establish contact with the turtles, which at that moment were laboring toward the main door, Juan managed to escape.

It was already six o'clock in the morning. He had sacrificed his hours of rest, and he had not been able to say even a word to Mr. Lockpez.

• 6 •

THAT day Juan was already at the building by one o'clock in the afternoon, two hours earlier than his usual schedule, because he had promised Miss Mary Avilés he would wash her windows. She lived alone on one of the top floors, and he considered her to be his fiancée.

Though she was originally from Cuba, Mary Avilés (actually María, according to her birth certificate) had been taken to Venezuela as a newborn baby by her parents; then the family moved to Miami, and while still a teenager (now she was twenty-seven) she had left home and never returned. She seldom talked about her parents, but when she did, she used to say she never wanted to see them ever again, not even at her funeral, which, by the way, she considered imminent. The truth is that, though by then Mary Avilés earned an excellent salary as a specialist at the Bronx Zoo, she did not work for her living but rather for her dying. She was not interested in staying in this world any longer. With six suicide attempts to prove it (and we have the records), her life was constantly on the brink of death.

At thirteen, Mary took a gun belonging to her father, a man of some influence in Miami's political arena, and shot herself in the chest. The bullet missed all her vital organs and in two weeks she was back at home, but suffering from the recriminatory glances of her entire family. At fourteen she took a whole bottle of the sleeping pills her mother used to take sparingly; and sleeping is what Mary Avilés did: for more than three days she slept without interruption. For her fifteenth birthday, the family, hoping that her *coming out* in society would put an end to these morbid intentions, organized for her a debutante ball that was both literally and figuratively high-flying, since this party was held on the rooftop terrace of the then-tallest building in Miami. Of course, Mary did not let such an opportunity go to waste. In her long and beautiful dress, all white lace, she jumped off into the void. This time it did seem her endeavors would not be bound to end in failure. But "the charming young lady," as the high-society pages of Miami's great Hispanic newspaper, *Diario de las Américas*, had heralded her, fell on top of an open trailer truck loaded with chickens, breaking through the chicken wire of the crates and causing a ruckus among the startled fowl, which, nonetheless, took advantage of the situation and escaped to freedom. . . . When Mary came to, thinking at first she had arrived in the afterworld — which she didn't believe in, by the way — she found herself surrounded by chickens, already passing through North Carolina. And that is how she reached New York.

After a few days in the city she jumped off the Brooklyn Bridge into the East River; the waters carried her to the harbor entrance, where an ocean liner approaching New York rescued her. It was teeming with tourists, who showered her with applause and placed a crown on her head, flashbulbs popping. They had mistaken her for the winner of the very popular "Swim Around Manhattan" competition. A few months later, Mary jumped off a skyscraper and fell on a vendor's umbrella, killing the poor woman underneath, who was selling hamburgers, and thanks to whom Mary escaped unscathed. Taken to court and without money to pay the fine, she was forced to seek employment. And that is how, always looking for an opportunity to leave this world, she began working at the zoo.

If it is true that Mrs. — or Miss — Avilés considered herself a "frustrated suicide" (and with plenty of reason), she had not resigned herself to live much longer. In this hope and with total conviction that she could never do away with herself intentionally, she had left her final destruction to fate, a kind of fate she intended to twist in her favor — or rather, in death's favor. For instance, at the zoo her responsibilities included feeding the fiercest and most treacherous beasts. Sometimes she asked the doorman to take her to the highest bluffs of the New Jersey Palisades, and pretending to look for a better spot for him to take her picture, she would step back to the very edge of the precipice. True, she was not jumping off, but if Juan had not been there to get hold of her at the last minute, she would have tumbled over the cliff. At the subway stop, with any innocent pretext (dropping her wallet, or a cigarette), she would jump down onto the rails in the hope of getting electrocuted by a spark from the third rail. . . . On many occasions she had pro-voked dramatic traffic accidents by crossing the street ignoring the DONT WALK sign, and though she always managed to come away unhurt, others were often injured. At other times she would frequent beer joints or walk through the worst neighbor-hoods, always hoping that, at least, she would get stabbed. People said that when Iberia, the Spanish airline, had a series of accidents, Mary Avilés began using that carrier. . . . In all cor-ners, drawers, and closets of her apartment she had planted potassium cyanide pills and other lethal substances, hoping one day to mistake them for aspirin or some other medication. On any of her tables or chairs one might find sharp razor blades, as well as a few guns (always cocked and loaded) on the bed or even inside the bathtub. Liquid Drano, rat poison, and roach killers could be found in the refrigerator. . . . As if all of these hazards weren't deadly enough, from the Bronx Zoo Mary Avilés had absconded with a rattlesnake, which slithered about the apartment making its bloodcurdling, hissing *whirrrrr.*

Her determination to make "fate" the accomplice to her demise led to her sixth, and last, frustrated suicide attempt. Truly upset by her lack of ability, despite incessant practice, in the art of ending her life, this time Mary Avilés planned her destruction in the following manner: she would swallow twenty Seconal tablets, set a lighted candle on the floor and a bucket of gasoline on a high chest of drawers; then tie a rope to the ceiling and hang herself, while at the same time tipping the bucket so the gasoline would spill and be ignited by the candle flame. In this way Miss Avilés would surely perish by burning, hanging, and overdosing, with the added advantage, as she wished, that nothing much of her person would remain, if any. But it seems that fate had decreed otherwise. The gasoline from the bucket came down with such violence that it doused the flame. Mary Avilés was left hanging but not gasping: the noose had slipped up around her chin, and since the tablets had put her to sleep, she could do nothing to facilitate her death. Forty-eight hours later, when she woke up, she found herself in a ridiculous position and alive as usual. Evidently death had refused to have anything to do with Mary Avilés, and she finally understood she was not going to succeed by forcing the situation. On the contrary, what she had to do was to allow death to take her by surprise. Of course, she also intended to elicit such a "surprise."

Precisely when Juan knocked at the door, Miss Avilés was trying to trick death again with one of her surprise plans. Even though Juan was coming to wash her windows, she had already started; without a protective belt there she was, polishing the glass from the outside, twenty-eight floors above street level. As her door was unlocked (another of Mary's tactics, in case a thief should drop by and maybe slit her throat), when the doorman knocked and there was no response, he came in. A cold chill went down his spine when he saw the beautiful girl outside the large window: her feet on the narrow ledge, one hand on top of the windowframe and the other cleaning the glass with a wet sponge. Miss Avilés greeted him in her usual dejected manner and insisted he sit near the window so she could hear him, for she had changed her mind and preferred to wash the windows herself this time.

Our doorman, aware of the rattlesnake, set a chair by the window and curled his feet up on the rungs while watching every corner.

The most wonderful aspect of Juan's relationship with Mary Avilés, even more than their supposed romance, was that she would very rarely interrupt his soliloquies. As far removed as possible from earthly concerns, Mary would only nod and mutter monosyllables, such as "hmmm," which she would often say in her Spanish mother tongue. Meanwhile our doorman, in English, would embark on his impassioned disquisitions, which made no sense at all. It was impossible to ascertain — as we indicated at the beginning — what exactly the young man intended to achieve with these lectures or monologues.

"Onward, onward! You are the chosen one!" Juan was telling himself now in a clearly audible voice. "Tell them they have to be reborn. Because life cannot be — "

"Don't mention life to me," Mary suddenly burst out, slipping back inside the apartment. She had finished the windows and stretched out on the sofa for a rest. Looking at the doorman, she said, in a different tone, "For my vacation I'd like to go to the Grand Canyon. They say it has the most wonderful cliffs in the world."

"I will try to go with you," the doorman told her, "but listen to me for a moment."

"I always listen to you," pleaded Mary, "you are the one who never listens to me, who never does what I ask."

"Precisely. Because I care for you."

"I know, but I don't want you to care for me, I want you to please me."

This kind of argument always stumped the doorman. His innate goodness, or his naiveté, made him try to please everybody, but he could never understand his supposed fiancée's suicidal wishes. On one occasion Mary Avilés had put a gun in his hands and said to him, "Shoot me in the head. Don't worry, it's only a game, it's not loaded." Fortunately Juan had checked the gun and seen the six bullets in the chamber. Sometimes, trying to awaken the subconscious violence that every human being (including our doorman) harbors, Mary would hand him sharp knives, ice picks, or even a sledgehammer, and then throw herself at his feet, screaming all sorts of insults at him. . . . The doorman would put aside all these weapons and resume his strange monologue. And Mary Avilés would be silent.

Why did Juan consider himself her fiancé? Maybe because almost all the inhabitants of the building thought so. Among them was the super's wife, who, in the worst English you ever heard, would tell anyone who would listen that she had seen the doorman and Miss Avilés embracing on the rooftop. Actually, what had happened was that Mary was walking backwards, trying to fall "accidentally" off the roof, and the doorman had caught her in time. Anyway, Juan also thought that, by his pretending to be engaged to her, Mary Avilés might regain an attachment to life in seeing that someone took a personal interest in her. As Mary Avilés was interested in absolutely nothing but her own destruction, she accepted his supposedly amorous confessions out of kindness, mainly to avoid undertaking the difficult task of disillusioning a young man in love.... And yet, in some mysterious way, between Mary and the doorman there developed a special connection, a sort of magic circle that, if not binding them to each other, at least brought them together. The two of them did not seem to be of this world, but they lived — rather, existed — as if this world and what it has to offer didn't interest them at all. Mary Avilés yearned in earnest to leave it; as for the doorman, he concentrated his efforts on trying to lead people to some still unknown, fantastic place he could not exactly locate, but which, he was sure, was not to be found in everyday reality.

And so it was that these two lonely and desperate people had found an affinity between them. Yes, the strange though disparate obsessions that consumed them somehow created a bond between them and, who knows, perhaps afforded them — we can't say for sure — some consolation.

Coming back to our story: In response to Mary's latest request, the doorman put aside for a moment his concerns about the lurking rattlesnake, uncurled his feet from the chair, and went to sit on the floor by the sofa where Mary Avilés was lying down staring at the ceiling. Juan softly put his head on her stomach and she, perhaps unconsciously, stroked his hair. Almost silently, Juan started to sob. Mary Avilés, still caressing him, closed her eyes.

"It's time for you to get back to your post," the young woman said to him after a while, as if she really cared about the doorman's not getting into trouble with the building management.

· 7 ·

BY six o'clock our doorman had already been at his post for three hours, opening and closing the big glass door. As always at this time, the tenants started coming down to take their pets for their evening walk.

The first to go out was Mr. Friedman, with his huge, sad-eyed dog, chewing (just like his master) some gooey confection. Inevitably, as he went through the door, Mr. Friedman bestowed upon the doorman his traditional piece of candy. Then came Dr. Rozeman with his three elegant lady-dogs, whose special ability continued to surprise Juan: instead of growling, these animals seemed to laugh and, topping this, they flashed such white, even teeth that their smiles looked definitely human. . . . Displaying his usual boisterousness, Mr. Lockpez appeared with his family and almost all his household menagerie: caged birds, cats and dogs pulling at their leashes, bugs in bottles, and even the two turtles, shell-to-shell, slowly ending the procession. It was already cool autumn weather, and one of the Lockpez boys was carrying a portable heater to keep the two doves and some of the insects warm, while the turtles were all wrapped in heavy pullovers that exposed only their heads and legs. Mr. Lockpez was very proud of these turtleneck sweaters his wife had fashioned.

Tipsy, but with her head held high, Brenda Hill sauntered down, her beauteous yellow cat bedecked with red and blue bows. A few seconds later, Miss Scarlett Reynolds appeared; this wealthy lady was too stingy to keep or feed a pet. Yet, not to be outdone by the rest of the tenants, every evening she took out and pulled along a large, stuffed, rag dog; each paw of the grotesque puppet was equipped with a little caster. Miss Reynolds asked the doorman for a quarter to make a phone call; for economic reasons she had had her own phone disconnected.

Behind this lady, and enveloped by the din of his huge suitcase-size radio, marched in Pascal Junior, the super's eldest son, with his five chihuahuas. He had so trained the tiny Mexican dogs that as they walked they danced along in time to the ear-splitting music. In fact, Pascal Junior was not listening to the same beat: his own large earphones were connected to the noise from a smaller cassette player attached to his belt.

Very solemn and dressed as if on his way to a formal reception, Arthur Makadam crossed the lobby, preceded as usual by his fastidiously groomed pet, an orangutan who kept jumping about and howling with joy. Mr. Makadam greeted the doorman politely, handed him a small envelope without meeting his eyes, and together with his hairy black beast, disappeared under the trees.

Next came Cassandra Levinson with her trained bear. This lady was such a political radical that, having read some Communist novel dramatizing the exploitation of bears in the circus by human beings, she made it her project, insofar as it was feasible for her, to repair this injustice. Therefore, she treated her pet bear as if it were a human being, taking it out for a walk without any leash. Idle gossips, particularly the super's wife, used to say that Mrs. Levinson even slept with the bear. . . . Then, to the doorman's surprise and delight, Mary Avilés came down, carrying her rattlesnake in a special cage that allowed one-way vision only: the snake could see out but no one could see in. Juan took it as an encouraging sign that Mary Avilés had decided to go for a walk, even though accompanied by a rattlesnake.

Not far behind her came one of the two Oscars with a huge bulldog following a terrified rabbit. Generally the two Oscars went out together, one with the rabbit and the other with the bulldog always threatening to pounce on the rabbit. But this time only one of them was doing the delicate maneuver of walking the two animals while keeping them separated, a feat that did not prevent him from glancing at our doorman's crotch. . . . When almost all the tenants had gone out, Mr. Stephen Warrem came down with his pet, a specimen quite unique in the world: Cleopatra. She was said to belong to a most royal Egyptian breed, and to be the direct descendant and last of her line of the sacred dogs from the palace of the great Egyptian queen after whom she had been named. Cleopatra's four legs were long and so delicate they did not look real, while her claws were like soft membranes. Her nervous body was very slender and ended in a scintillating plume, while her neck was even longer than her legs, her snout delicate, her ears pure velvet, and her eyes violet. Her shiny coat was jet black and her eyes, besides their unique color, seemed to radiate a disturbing glow. Always facing front, with head held high and nose tilted up, she walked in regal and solemn glory. One would think she was a mythological creature. She had never ever barked, as the Warrems confessed and all the rest of the neighbors confirmed, neither had she ever growled or whined or, least of all, wagged her tail. She usually slept standing up. Except for Mr. and Mrs. Warrem, at whom she glanced once in a while, all haughtiness and disdain, she had never allowed anyone to touch her. While the tenants and their pets gathered in the lobby, she would not come out of the elevator. That was the reason why the Warrems would wait until everybody had gone, or until there was nobody in the lobby, to take their quite remarkable dog — and their only pet — out for a walk. According to confirmed information, the animal had cost them a million dollars in a sensational auction held five years previously in Cairo. It was true that Cleopatra belonged to no known breed of dog, and there seemed to be no other like her. Obviously it was utterly inconceivable that this dog could be mated with any other living dog. So there was no possibility at all of continuing her line. Each time Cleopatra passed him in the lobby our doorman looked at her with strange apprehension, as well as inexplicable awe. The dog, for her part, would simply wait for Juan to open the door and then, aloof and regal, she would exit, followed by Mr. or Mrs. Warrem, who, despite their fashionable and expensive attire, looked like mere attendants.

Juan was still mesmerized by Cleopatra when a chorale of trills and birdsongs right there in the lobby brought him back to reality. It was Mr. Skirius, who had been delayed working on his last invention. Walter Skirius walked into the lobby, jubilant, with a dozen birds of different sizes, multicolor plumage, and various singing registers fluttering around his head. As he went by the doorman, Mr. Skirius sort of bowed to him, and the birds trilled in unison as if they, too, were greeting Juan; immediately they flew down to their master's shoulders while the inventor, waving one hand, signaled goodbye to the doorman. It didn't take long for Juan to understand that these birds were just another mechanical invention of this electronic genius, about whom we'll have more to say later on.

As the warbling of the mechanical birds was dying out, the doorman took out the envelope Arthur Makadam had given him.

· 8 ·

ARTHUR Makadam had spent most of his fortune on what he liked to call his "quest for love." Apparently he had never found it, for he continued to squander whatever meager funds he still possessed. He had traveled almost all over the world and had had affairs with women of various ages, races, cultures, and faiths. But all of these affairs — some of them not at all unworthy — had failed to provide any lasting fulfillment. Nor even a moment of pleasure intense enough to produce a memory whose evocation would have provided him with a measure of solace and joy. Now that evidently he was no longer young, nor even a man "of a certain age" who, by means of his personal qualities, could seduce a woman, Arthur Makadam felt lonelier and more desperate. He was an old man — though still trim and with an impressive mane he himself dyed black — and pleasure came to him only through the modern matchmaker — money, whose miracles outnumber those of all the matchmakers of old combined. His battle against time, like that of all those who refuse to give up and concede that time always wins, acquired with each day more pathetic proportions. His suits were progressively of brighter and brighter colors — green, yellow, or even brilliant orange; he would wear heavy makeup and dark glasses, dye his mustache, polish his nails, and affect a youthful gait so unnatural that it made him look either stiff or bouncy. Everything about him underlined not his lost youth but an old age, which had become a cruel caricature. And as if this natural deterioration wasn't enough to discourage Mr. Makadam's insistent pose as Don Juan, he had also been ravaged by venereal diseases, which, though conquered, had left their marks, along with scars from more than a few extortions and blackmailing incidents with some females who were truly experts in these matters. And to top it all, and this seemed to be the coup de grâce to his adventurous life, Mr. Makadam became impotent. The end of a career in debauchery, false arrogance, and desolation seemed to be coming to an end: but at that moment Mr. Makadam discovered, or thought he was the one to discover, that true pleasure is not in the receiver but in the giver and that, all in all, authentic sexual pleasure does not mean to experience pleasure but to give it to others, that is, to the oversized women (and it is fair to say, so generously endowed) whom Mr. Makadam preferred. But how to please these women, these very experienced women, when the main weapon could not be readied for battle? And it is fair to say also that by means of a very proficient masturbatory exercise, Mr. Makadam could still achieve the pleasure of orgasm. The first thing Mr. Makadam did was to consult experts in sexual matters. He visited almost every New York establishment listed under *Sex Books and Supplies* that offered all kinds of lubricants, vibrators, mechanical phalluses, plastic dildos, and a vast catalog of erotic merchandise generally referred to as "sexual aids." Properly equipped with all these tools, Mr. Makadam began his new kind of erotic life. And it must be said that his new "instruments" were very useful. With so many years of practice, Mr. Makadam knew prodigiously well how to excite any woman; only at the moment of climax was he forced to resort to his "gadgets," which, precisely because they were *mechanical*, very seldom failed him. In this way, the spasms of the "lady-guest of the day" could coincide with Mr. Makadam's self-induced climax. In all fairness it should be said that, by means of effective lighting and acoustics, Mr. Makadam was able to create such a charged, hallucinatory atmosphere that none of these women ever suspected that anything except Arthur Makadam's own virile member could be producing in them such extraordinary pleasure. Ironically, it was just when Mr. Makadam's potency reached its lowest ebb that he acquired a considerable reputation as an extremely virile, indefatigable, and eager-to-please lover. The news, of course, reached Brenda Hill through the super's wife. Immediately she managed, under some pretense, to extend to him an invitation to her apartment in order to avail herself of his services. But Mr. Makadam could not secretly, and without being noticed, take along all his sexual paraphernalia, so he opted for inviting Miss Hill to his apartment. And at the point when Arthur Makadam seemed on the verge of victory, Brenda Hill sat up, stretched forward, and fondled with disgust and outrage a perfect pair of rubber testicles — the rest still inside her. Brenda Hill slapped Mr. Makadam, calling him a fake, a fraud, and also a traitor. The slaps had the effect of exciting him even more. Still, because the insults greatly demoralized him, he tried to excuse himself by claiming he was not feeling up to par and promised her "the real thing" the following week. Brenda Hill agreed to this, and after warning him that if he failed she would sue him for sexual assault, stomped out. That whole week was agonizing for Mr. Makadam. He knew, from years of experience, both the danger and the public humiliation that could follow if he left a woman unfulfilled in bed. Theft, beatings, betrayal, and even attempted murder could be forgiven: anything but leaving her ungratified. On the other hand, and quite apart from the threat of public disgrace and court proceedings, the mere idea of having left her unfulfilled was a dishonor that Mr. Makadam, who had dedicated his life to the sexual act, could not possibly accept. . . . This time, instead of visiting cheap 42nd Street sex shops, he called true experts to his aid: pimps and legendary hookers who lived in veritable palaces. On the eve of his appointment with Brenda Hill, Arthur Makadam came home with a gigantic and so well-trained ape that even our doorman bowed to him. . . . That night, all perfumed and dressed in Mr. Makadam's clothes, and protected by the utter darkness Mr. Makadam had very gradually created, the orangutan was able to bring Brenda Hill to ecstasy, while right at their side, Mr.

Makadam masturbated quickly, breathing heavily and regaling her with voluptuous utterances. After the coupling, the animal went right into a closet, as expected. The lights were back, and Brenda Hill asked right away for a repeat performance. But Mr. Makadam, pleading a previous appointment with another lady, got dressed and accompanied his guest to the door. There they parted like true lovers. . . . Everything would have worked perfectly, both for Mr. Makadam and for Brenda Hill, except that the ape had taken a fancy to the lady. And one night, when Brenda was reaching her climax at the same instant, of course, as Arthur Makadam and the orangutan, the ape, at the peak of his pleasure, began to screech in such a simian fashion that no matter how carried away the lady was by her own feelings, she could not fail to notice that such screeching was not produced by a human throat. Brenda held fast to her partner, and introduced her hands under Mr. Makadam's suit, immediately realizing why he always wanted to make love fully clothed, white gloves included: underneath all that expensive apparel there was nothing but the thick, hairy chest of a rutting monkey. . . . This time her outrage and her threats reached the limit; she went berserk. While the orangutan was still moaning with pleasure, Brenda stood up and, after beating Mr. Makadam repeatedly, solemnly swore she would bring him to court on charges of bestiality and sadism. Mr. Makadam tried to appease her momentarily by writing her a check for a thousand dollars, assuring her their next rendezvous would be *au naturel* and absolutely satisfactory. Still fuming, Mrs. Hill asked him why didn't they have this "next rendezvous" right then and there. Makadam, apologizing and again pleading a previous appointment, postponed it until the following week. Reluctantly, Brenda agreed, saying she would put her legal claim on hold until she saw the results of their next meeting.

It was then that Mr. Makadam noticed our handsome doorman, and slipped him an envelope with an invitation to his apartment. . . . And now Juan, dressed in Mr. Makadam's best suit and scented with his best cologne, with true euphoria (that we won't deny) found himself making love to Mrs. Hill, whose cries of delight mingled with the monkey's moans coming from the closet where he was being kept by force, and with Arthur Makadam's groans as he masturbated, laughing and crying at the same time. Standing in the dark, close to the entwined couple, he thought: "Now my reputation will definitely be restored!" But at that moment, when Mrs. Hill was reaching the heights of yet another orgasm, the orangutan, in a fit of wild jealousy, broke through the door that held him captive and leapt between the doorman and Mrs. Hill, producing such thundering shrieks that the whole building shook.

In no time, running down the elegant hallways, we saw our half-dressed doorman (who had quickly sneaked out); then Brenda Hill, in her panties; closely followed by a big ape dressed as a man, whom she was threatening to take to court; and after them, Mr. Makadam, stark naked, and alas, *bald!* (he had fooled everybody, even us), still trying to stop the stampede.

Brenda Hill did file suit as promised (bestiality, mental cruelty, sadism, sexual assault . . .) against Arthur Makadam and against the orangutan, but that very night they both vanished, each on his separate way.

· 9 ·

IT'S true, they've disappeared. But this doesn't mean that they're dead or in jail. They are simply in another dimension now, on their own planet. Because they were extraterrestrials."

That was how Mr. Walter Skirius, the inventor, calmly explained the whole thing to our doorman.

"That must be it," asserted Juan not only because, as a doorman, he could never contradict the tenants, but because he liked to support Mr. Skirius's theories for being so daring, as most of them were.

"Nowhere in the history of zoology," pronounced Mr. Skirius, "will you find a natural ape with the intelligence and loyalty displayed by Mr. Makadam's orangutan. Obviously, he is an android or electronic robot made by beings from another planet."

"It's quite probable," nodded our doorman, and with an earnest expression he got ready to listen to another strange scientific hypothesis or a long discourse about interplanetary beings.

We should hasten to make clear that Mr. Walter Skirius was not one of those typical blustering technocrats who are always inventing new outlandish spaceships or mind-reading machines. Mr. Skirius was really an inventor par excellence, a real devotee of invention, a true believer in science and a constant researcher. Perhaps for that reason our doorman felt especially drawn to the man. Deep down they shared certain traits: each was seeking or hoping for something that could surpass even his own established goals. Thus our doorman saw in this unbalanced, obsessed man a potential militant for his own cause.

And the same thing happened to Mr. Skirius regarding our doorman. Juan was the only human being with enough patience to listen to him, and Mr. Skirius saw in the doorman a disciple in need of enlightenment.

Juan was already familiar with most of Mr. Skirius's inventions — among them, of course, the electronic birds and other kinds of mechanical animals. He had also invented a television set where one could simultaneously see on the same screen all the channels, mixing the most incongruous scenes, actions, and periods. . . . Without moving away from the telephone, by pressing button #7, Mr. Skirius could open the door to his apartment; with another number he could close it, and with yet another he could bolt its double lock. He could turn a knob on his radio to start the washing machine and flush the toilet at the same time; according to the level of pressure he exerted, he could set in motion the record or CD player, the radio or the tape recorder, in any order he chose.

The combination lock on the front door was attached to an electronic device that, as the door opened or closed, would turn the house lights on or off. And from the bed, of course also wired electronically, a specific pressure point in the mattress would light the oven, turn on the automatic vacuum cleaner, or even open or close the terrace windows.

Mr. Skirius's most famous invention, the neon clothespin, became widely used though he could never patent it. It was said to have prevented serious accidents when country housewives hung their wash out to dry during the day and took it in after dark. Besides his many neon gadgets, Mr. Skirius had also invented books for hermits — volumes with phosphorescent letters that enabled anyone removed from civilization to read into the night. One of his best-known inventions (endorsed even by Ed Koch, then Mayor of New York City) was the magnetized headpiece for drug addicts. Considering the tremendous number of drug addicts in New York — then and now — who often have trouble staying vertical, Mr. Skirius's great achievement was to forcibly keep those tottering masses on their feet once they wore the magnetic helmet, which, by always pointing North, held them perpetually upright. Evidently, our doorman noticed this was not totally original: with the helmet on, they looked like full-size replicas of those wooden dolls we had as children, with a rounded bottom that would always return them to their upright position, even when we tried to make them stand on their heads. . . . It is true that now, in 1992, the magnetic helmet has fallen into disuse, discarded by drug addicts who don't consider themselves really zonked out as long as they can stand at all. Besides, it was outlawed by the police, for whom this invention made it nearly impossible to distinguish a drugged person from a corpse, particularly since many murderers, as a cover-up, had taken to dressing up their victims with the famous helmet. Sometimes the only recognizable difference was the stench of the decomposing bodies. . . . With this string of successes already behind him, Mr. Skirius was now working on a "premature snow melter," which caused snow to sublime (or vaporize without melting) before it reached the ground, using high-tech laser beams. These inventions for the public benefit were fascinating indeed, but the innovations he had created and put into practice for his personal use were even more astounding.

According to his theory, the human body was only a clumsy machine jammed with organs either constantly overworked or vulnerable, open to all sorts of breakdowns and malfunctions: disease, intoxication, indigestion, new waves of epidemics, extreme heat or cold, and — oh! — aging. Mr. Skirius intended to replace almost every natural body part with perfect and powerful mechanical replicas. He had already had one of his legs amputated at the first sign of arthritis and replaced with one made of reinforced steel, so perfect in structure and performance that only the slightest limp could be detected. One of his hands was not natural either, along with a large part of his small intestine, one of his lungs, his two kidneys, his hair, both testicles, his prostate, and one eye, which had stopped functioning as such, though this is a secret between Skirius and us.

Precisely at that moment Mr. Skirius began encouraging our doorman to cut off his left arm, the one he always used to open the door.

"You use that arm so many times a day, it must be sore all the time," Walter Skirius was saying. "If it were mechanical, not only would you feel no pain, you could move it faster."

"That's true," our doorman answered. He was not yet convinced he should cut off his arm, but he was still considering the possibility, not because he looked forward to the idea of becoming a one-armed doorman, but because following Mr. Skirius's suggestions would create a spiritual bond with the inventor and perhaps then Juan could win him over to his own cause: the joint search for that marvelous door Juan was so eagerly trying to find, without knowing how.

"Actually," Mr. Skirius went on with conviction, "we are lowly animals condemned to death and putrefaction," and at this point, by pressing an electronic gadget connected to his vocal cords, which he had implanted on his chest, he gave his voice a tragic, almost desperate, tone: "We are still so remote from the ideal perfection," he added while manipulating another of his gadgets, this time the one near his neck. His voice then became absolutely serene: "But some day all these difficulties will be overcome. Why, for instance, should we have to keep implanting this extraneous equipment when we could become better instruments ourselves?" And with a slight adjustment of his emotion-control box, Mr. Skirius's voice took on a positive intonation: "No! In order to fly, why should we need to travel in those dangerous flying contraptions, when we could fly or leap or swim at greater speeds than any of these machines? Do you really know what it means to spend your entire life inside an automobile?" And at the press of another button, Mr. Skirius's voice became emotional and intimate: "Do you know what it means to be always at the mercy of other people's madness just because they are driving ahead of you or behind you? We waste a lifetime waiting for the green light, or crawling through a tunnel, or on a plane, waiting for permission to land or take off, not to mention being stranded because of delays and schedule changes. Just figure out how much time is left for you to live, and you will see it's not much. And the little time that is left over is wasted on myriad stupid, if unavoidable, chores like washing clothes, preparing meals, opening and closing doors, cleaning the house, going to the dentist, brushing our hair, flushing the toilet . . ."

"But you have already eliminated many of these inconveniences," offered the doorman in a lighter tone, seeing that Mr. Skirius, after pressing another button, was on the verge of tears.

"Still, I haven't done enough! I haven't fulfilled my dream yet!" blurted out Mr. Skirius, adding enough wattage to his voice to startle Mrs. Levinson, who had been eavesdropping from the hallway throughout this strange dialogue.

"It's not enough!" Mr. Skirius proclaimed again in his metallic voice, as if possessed by his inner devils, and then began pacing the great hall as fast as his mechanisms would allow while counting out the miracles that the powers of Invention still held in store for mankind, miracles he himself intended to realize: metal legs that would no longer smart from blows to the shins, as human legs do all the time; fingers that, once they had become beautiful steel tentacles, would no longer be subject to cold, to burns, to being caught in doors, pricked by thorns, twisted or smashed, as they now are. *"And, oh, my friend, what do you say about the eyes, so fragile and yet so indispensable? . . ."*

At this point Mr. Skirius stopped and, facing the doorman again, recovered his measured, grave tone: "The eyes, perhaps the most precious part of our body, are so vulnerable that a blowing wind can cloud them over, and a stray spark can blind them forever!"

"It's so true, so true," agreed our doorman, whose eyes felt irritated every day after eight hours under the strong blaze of the big chandelier in the lobby.

"And what about the throat? As sensitive to hot liquids as to ice cream, to spicy or salty foods, to humidity, to dust . . ."

"Very true, sir," again volunteered our doorman, thinking that what this man needed to guide him on the right path toward wider possibilities was a good leader, and that he, Juan, would be the one to show him the way.

"And think about the nails!" now cried Mr. Skirius in his strange, metallic voice while tapping the glass panes of the great door with one of his artificial nails. "Do you know of anything worse than an ingrown toenail? And what do you think about your teeth, if you have any left, symbols of our aging and source of recurring pain, expense, and trouble? And what about your tongue? One of mankind's most precious organs, and yet so exposed to dangers from the surrounding world, from insect bites to germ particles in the air, to contaminating kisses . . ."

"I agree," responded Juan while Mr. Skirius, his enthusiasm rising, continued circling around our doorman. "And did you know — " Mr. Skirius paused, tapping the doorman's chest with his mechanical steel index finger. "Did you know the tongue can also be replaced by a perfect organ, not a crude copy, but something even more dynamic, lighter, ultrasensitive, and long-lasting? Did you know there are thousands of flavors unknown to our rudimentary palate?"

"Why, no, I didn't know."

"Well, now you know!" At this point Mr. Skirius was already screaming, and in a paroxysm of fervor and creative exultation, facing the doorman directly, he added: "Look, this is my latest invention," and then opened his mouth as wide as his jaws would allow to offer a better view.

The doorman was astonished to see that the inventor had succeeded in replacing his tongue with some finely crafted, flexible, and durable metal plates.

"Incredible!" Juan cried. Mr. Skirius, overcome by his small triumph, wanted to show Juan that his brand-new tongue, and even his new throat, now platinum-coated, were not only capable of enunciating in any tone of voice, but also of singing and, yes, with a more powerful projection than any living tenor or baritone. To prove his point, he began to sing one of the most difficult arias from *Il Trovatore*, and the enormous luxury building shook. That voice — so potent, sensitive, fresh, so well modulated — was truly extraordinary. It rose and fell with such musicality that even Miss Reynolds, immersed in her financial computations, had to stop for a minute. And the Pietris respectfully (and this was the ultimate proof of his power) lowered the volume of their cassette players. But then, suddenly, Mr. Skirius's throat, instead of producing exquisite arias, began pouring out bursts of flames. A green fire, as if propelled by a torch, almost burned off Juan's eyelashes. Mr. Skirius desperately lifted his mechanical arm, seeking the control panel on his chest, but the flames kept growing in intensity. Something in that mechanical complex that was now Mr. Skirius's body had evidently misfired and provoked a short circuit. Like a frenzied dragon, Walter Skirius jumped about the great hall while the terrified doorman followed him trying to offer some help, to no avail.

At that moment Cassandra Levinson appeared, wielding the building's fire extinguisher. Wonderfully calm and collected, she put out the fire in no time. When she was through, all that was left of Mr. Skirius was a tangle of charred cables and bones.

"Let's go up to my apartment and call the police," said Cassandra Levinson, taking our dazed doorman by the hand.

10

ONCE upstairs, Mrs. Levinson notified the police, and offered Juan a drink.

"They are coming to pick up the body," she said, referring to the heap of cables lying on the lobby floor. "Really, his death doesn't surprise me. Mr. Skirius was the ultimate expression of the prevalent mechanicism that is the product of absurd, imperialist technology," pontificated Mrs. Levinson and, in a flash, the whole incident was forgotten, and she returned to her single topic of conversation with the doorman: his political rehabilitation.

To understand Cassandra Levinson one needs to know that, besides being a member of the Communist party in the United States (a right no one disputes) and a professor of political science at Columbia University with a salary of $80,000 a year, she was also a fanatic and front-line instrument of the Cuban dictator. Our doorman, after seventeen years of hunger and humiliation under the Cuban Communist system, had fled the country on a small boat. Cassandra Levinson had imposed upon herself, for philosophical, moral, and even "humane" reasons, the task of convincing our doorman that he had made a mistake and that what he had left behind was nothing short of paradise.

"You could still be pardoned," she said in a sententious manner, both authoritative and understanding. "You are young. You surely did not know what you were doing. And you are neither a hardened criminal, nor one of the *lumpenproletariat*, nor an exploiter of the people. You do not need to stay here."

Juan was wondering whether she considered herself an exploiter or a criminal, since she would not leave this country for Cuba either. Cassandra Levinson did not stop talking, and her sermon reminded the doorman of the same words he had heard, the same hypocritical rhetoric, from the Cuban Ministry of the Interior when — after he had taken political asylum in 1980 at the Peruvian Embassy and had nearly starved to death (together with another 10,800 Cuban refugees) — government agents were trying to convince everybody not to leave the country for the sake of "social and moral principles. . . ."

Hearing the same words again now from the professor, our doorman could not help but feel irritated, in spite of his usual deference to all the tenants. After all, those agents who tried to convince him to stay in Cuba had to remain there themselves and suffer, perhaps to a lesser degree, the outrages of the regime, which were intolerable for any human being. All in all, Juan concluded, Cassandra Levinson was considerably more evil and immoral than even the system's executioners. She was profiting from a hell she did not have to suffer.

"Your case can be reviewed, I am sure," the professor said encouragingly, now addressing him in a familiar tone.

Every year she would go to Cuba two or three times. She stayed at the best hotels, at no cost to her, and besides being "informed" of the latest necessary "orientations," she would engage in such intense sexual activity that upon her return she became a most proper and respectable lady, an almost devout practitioner of sexual abstinence.

"Your objections to the regime cannot be that strong. . . ."

While Cassandra Levinson stayed in Cuba, carried away by an antidiscriminatory attitude (actually a backlash that turned her into a reverse racist), she slept only with black men and, for the sake of political camaraderie, occasionally with members of the Central Committee for the Defense of the Revolution, no matter what their race.

"I am positive you could be rehabilitated and allowed to go back to your country. . . ."

She usually arrived on the island with several suitcases bursting with handkerchiefs, deodorants, pantyhose, perfume, jockey shorts, bathing suits, and hundreds of other coveted articles that are either rationed or nonexistent in Cuba, but which she could buy for next to nothing in the States. Laden with all these luxuries, this militant woman, though in her fifties, would entice young men who, in the hope of getting a new pair of socks or a T-shirt, would be willing to bring her to multiple orgasms.

"And even though you might not want to go back, and I can understand how difficult it is to adjust to the austerity demanded by a country carrying on a revolution, you could work here for its cause, you could stop being a traitor to your country. . . ."

"I left Cuba to stop being a traitor," the doorman said in the same restrained tone he used each time the dialogue reached this point (it always did), and he had to repeat the same reply.

It obviously irritated Cassandra Levinson that her words, no less than direct quotes from the *Manual for the Perfect Communist* (published by Ediciónes del Norte, in which she was a stockholder), had been unable to bring back into the fold that poor lost sheep for whom she seemed to feel some affection.

She then went over to her caged pet, a very jealous bear. It was very clear that her long conversation with the doorman was making the animal restless, and it began to growl. With her bony hands she caressed its muzzle and all over its black coat, which was dyed. The bear stopped growling and Cassandra resumed her ideological siege.

"Don't you see," she said to the doorman, now in a formal tone, "how miserable your life really is, always opening the door for people who look down on you and consider you inferior?"

"I also open the door for you," countered the doorman, "and I don't think you look down on me. Even though they may not appreciate me, I appreciate them, and I want to help them. I want to open not only that door, but other doors as well. . . ."

"Pure bourgeois idealism!" protested Cassandra Levinson.

"The only way to really help mankind is to join the cause of the working classes."

"I belong to the working classes, and where I come from, according to you, that battle has already been won."

"You are all confused. The enemies of the system over there filled your head with weird notions."

"Over there the only thing the enemies of the system can fill is the prisons. Freedom — "

"Don't talk to me about freedom!" Now Mrs. Levinson was offended. "You don't even know what the word means!"

"If I didn't know, how come we have been discussing it for a long time without any problems?" the doorman objected in a conciliatory tone, and tried to end the conversation on the pretext that he had to go back to his post at the door.

"Yes, go and serve your masters," Cassandra Levinson sneered, but instead of letting him go, she sat down next to him on the sofa and took his hands while looking at him intensely. Mrs. Levinson apparently thought that her intense, militant gaze had hypnotic powers and that in no time the doorman would fall at her feet, converted to Marxism. But it didn't happen that way. Once again Juan tried to excuse himself and withdraw. "I must sweep the lobby and clean the carpet. I am really sorry about Mr. Skirius's death," he added sadly.

"Mr. Skirius was a victim of this capitalist consumer society," Mrs. Levinson started again. "In Cuba this accident would never have happened."

"You are right," the doorman agreed, "but there, he would not have existed either."

And seeing that for a moment Cassandra was at a loss for words, Juan bowed and left her apartment.

ONCE in the hallway, our doorman blamed himself for the way he had treated Mrs. Levinson. It was not that he thought she was right; of course she wasn't. But that was not important at all. Muttering, he blamed himself for not having been able to bring the conversation toward other topics closer to his own cause. Instead of drawing closer to her, he had only managed to increase the distance between them.

Back at his post, his face darkened at the thought that, one way or the other, his efforts to befriend the tenants and lead them to the Great Door had failed completely till now. None of them, not Mr. Lockpez, Mary Avilés, Mr. Makadam, or Roy Friedman, much less Cassandra Levinson — well, or Mr. Skirius, of course — had been won over to his cause.

The tenants were now coming back with their pets. Joseph Rozeman and his bunch of female dogs smiled mechanically at him. Miss Reynolds asked Juan for the customary quarter, and without saying even a word of thanks, her nose up in the air, she went by with her rag dog. John Lockpez tapped Juan's nose as he passed by and rushed upstairs with his menagerie. Juan kept on opening and closing the door, and greeting everybody politely. . . . Suddenly, an egg hurled forcefully from the hallway exploded in his face. Obviously Pascal Junior or his sister was at it again. Juan would have to complain to the super, who, being the kids' father, would naturally not do anything about it. For a while, until the parade of tenants ended, Juan could not leave his post.

Instinctively, he wiped his face with his hand and then, as best he could, with his handkerchief. But he could not alter the expression of sadness that had come over his face. He had an irrational fear: he felt sure that if that sadness left him, an even greater feeling of desolation would then take hold of him. It was just then that he felt something wet touching his hand. He looked down and was dumbfounded to see Cleopatra, the last specimen of that rare and extinguished race, licking him softly, while Stephen Warrem watched the scene in astonishment.

"It must be the egg they threw at me," the embarrassed doorman tried to explain. "It is not my fault, sir, it's the super's children. They are always pestering me."

"Oh, not at all," Mr. Warrem said, somewhat lost in his thoughts and rather confused, while he patiently waited for Cleopatra to finish.

In his distress, the doorman was about to pull away his hand, when Mr. Warrem stopped him.

"Don't move!" he said. "She knows what she is doing."

"Do you think so?" the doorman asked sheepishly.

"Didn't anybody tell you that Cleopatra is the most intelligent dog in the world," and he lowered his voice to say the word *dog* as if the dog might understand it and be offended, "that I paid a fortune for her, and that every movement she makes is perfectly calculated? She is incapable of an impulsive action, and even less an expression of trust and affection of this magnitude toward anyone, not even toward me. I am amazed! You . . . she doesn't even know you, an ordinary doorman (no offense meant, just a fact), and she has licked your hand!"

"It was the egg, I am sure," Juan answered modestly, trying to justify himself.

"That is sheer nonsense! The *egg*! Are you suggesting that Cleopatra is a common chicken-coop thief? If your hands are unclean, that is your problem, and you ought to avoid it. But if Cleopatra licks your hands, it must be for a serious reason that I urgently need to investigate."

Meanwhile, Cleopatra had finished licking and, recovering her regal demeanor, started to walk away.

Mr. Warrem was forced to mutter a quick goodbye to the doorman, not without adding that Cleopatra's doctor (he always avoided saying "veterinarian") would surely like to ask him a few questions. He was not really afraid the doorman might have a contagious disease, but in order to be sure, it was better that Cleopatra's specialist examine him.

"Please try to be available all day tomorrow." And Mr. Warrem rushed after Cleopatra, who was already going into the elevator. But all of a sudden he turned around and with swift savoir faire slipped into the doorman's breast pocket a $100 bill.

· 12 ·

THE Warrems' sumptuous yacht was gliding majestically through the waters of the Atlantic. On its deck was a resonant pipe organ, with a world-famous organist playing to perfection (and woe to him if he didn't) a Bach toccata. Apparently there were only two creatures in the audience for this superb performance: Cleopatra and our doorman.

This was the third time Juan had been invited to spend his day off with the Warrems. But today, just as on the two previous occasions, it was not precisely with the Warrems that he spent his day off, but with their one-of-a-kind dog.

Since the afternoon when Cleopatra had licked Juan's hand, Mr. Warrem and his whole aristocratic family had been thrown into an unbearable confusion. Her behavior was the source of their puzzlement, and no matter how hard they tried, they could not reach any acceptable conclusion. Never had Cleopatra done anything like this to either of her masters, not even to their children, who had tried so often to win her over with toys and games, words of affection, and offers of exotic morsels. In return they had gotten nothing but scornful looks or even discouraging growls. As for Mr. Warrem, he watched over this strange animal with devotion and even with fear. In his vast circle of contacts, he had never met any other being, except for Cleopatra, who had not become subservient to him. For this reason, after that rare encounter between her and the doorman, Mr. Warrem decided to leave for Egypt (even at the cost of missing a cocktail party that included the Governor of

New York) to hold a conference with the director of the exclusive and powerful firm that had sold him this unique specimen.

The director was as baffled as Mr. Warrem. Neither Cleopatra nor any of her most distant ancestors had any record of ever displaying such an "intimate show of affection" with their masters or anyone else and, of course, much less with a simple doorman.

"Well, now," concluded the head of the prestigious canine concern, "there could be only two possible reasons for her strange behavior: a form of mental imbalance, which is almost impossible for her breed, or a very obscure motivation worthy of study."

The next day, Mr. Warrem returned to New York accompanied by the chief veterinarian of the powerful company, who immediately subjected Cleopatra to a serious examination. The first alternative had to be virtually discarded, he explained, because the canine's physical and mental condition was superb. Only the second possibility remained. All of Cleopatra's future reactions to the doorman had to be secretly monitored. Mr. Warrem needed *to provoke* contacts between The Divine One (as they called the dog) and our doorman.

Naturally, both Mr. and Mrs. Warrem were discomfited at the prospect that not only The Divine One but they themselves had to seek the company of a doorman "who is not even American" (those were Mr. Warrem's exact words, which we have on tape). So, in order to avoid the paparazzi, always thirsty for unusual gossip items about the lives of the rich and famous, they decided that the best strategy was to have Cleopatra meet with the doorman on their family yacht. More precisely, to include the doorman in the customary sea cruises that the wealthy family enjoyed. So, weather permitting, the Warrems and a select group of friends (all socially prominent, well-known personalities, such as a senator or two, a governor, the Mayor of New York City, a district attorney, and an occasional movie star) would sail out on a weekly cruise, during which, like it or not, the big attraction was the nonpareil Cleopatra.

There was only one thing in the vast world at her disposal that seemed to move her: the sound of organ music. To please her, the Warrems always booked the most distinguished organists. As a result, Cleopatra's musical education had reached a high degree of refinement. Her ear for music, naturally quite acute, had developed to such a degree that she could detect — and react violently against — the slightest anomaly in the rendition or even in the fingering of a piece. The performers in fact were at risk and had to watch every step (or rather, every note): a wrong note had cost several performers their lives (including the famous Margot Rubinstein, whose body was limp and lifeless by the time she was extricated from Cleopatra's dainty fangs). This incident caused quite a stir; even *The New York Times* picked it up. The closest relatives (mother and husband) of the deceased organist could only be silenced with a compensation of over a million dollars. People still say that Mother Teresa had attended that concert, and in order to assuage her religious scruples the Warrems had to donate half a million dollars to her charitable organizations — even the Warrems, wealthy as they were, could ill afford Cleopatra's musical refinements.

However, when the artist performed the music well (as was most often the case, fortunately), an extraordinary feeling of fulfillment and contentment suffused the animal, even when a few minutes earlier, by means of her ferocious stare, she had forced the distinguished audience to retreat in silence to the refuge of their cabins or to the deck stairs. Then she would stretch her body across the deck, her front legs fully extended, head on the floor, and eyes fixed on the starry sky. It was only at night, with no lights on deck except starlight, that Cleopatra would immerse herself in the sweet harmonies of the organ.

Tonight, and this was most unusual, while a magnificent composition by Bach reverberated for the third time across the surrounding ocean, Cleopatra was not alone on deck. Against the railing, and also in bliss, stood our doorman in full uniform, eyes lost in the distance. . . . Below deck, leaning against the hatch stairs but not daring to visibly raise their heads, the

Warrems, the Mayor of New York, two district attorneys, Meryl Streep, and the Dean of Saint Patrick's Cathedral, together with the preeminent veterinarians, were all holding their breath and surreptitiously contemplating the scene.

The brilliant organist went from the toccatas to the fugues, from the fugues to the preludes, from the preludes to the fantasies, from the fantasies to the cantatas and chorales. . . . The yacht continued gliding smoothly through the phosphorescent waters. The moon rose serenely from starboard, so full and indescribably beautiful that no words — only its contemplation — could do it justice. The melody filled every corner, indistinguishable at times from the sound of the waves and sometimes cresting over them. Cleopatra listened oblivious to the world, glancing up at the stars or at the doorman, who once in a while would take out his notebook as usual and write something in it. Below the bridge, the hosts, guests, and servants stood together in speechless awe, as if they had no right to listen; the music belonged to Cleopatra, the doorman, and the sea.

At well past midnight the dog got up, and paying no attention to anyone, went below slowly, just as she had done at the previous concerts.

At that moment, the performance ended.

THE guests, escorted by their hosts and attended by the servants, could now move up to the deck. The lights came on and the dance party began to the rhythms of a large orchestra. Everybody was congratulating the Warrems for their "fabulous" (that was the exact word they used) Cleopatra. The Warrems, however, as well as the noted veterinarians, were still stunned. So far they hadn't been able to find the slightest clue as to Cleopatra's strange attitude toward the doorman. On the other hand, the dog had not come close to Juan again, though she had not rejected him. To make matters worse, a bone-chilling wind was visibly riffling the guests' precious furs: sure proof to the Warrems that winter was upon them. Very soon their cruise season would have to end.

Mr. Warrem led Juan discreetly to a corner, gave him another $100 bill, and informed him that for a while his services would not be required. Making an attempt to refuse the money, the doorman proposed that, if they worked together, they could perhaps find a solution, a "way out" he knew of. Yes, he was almost sure there was a door, and that . . . But Mr. Warrem cut short Juan's confused words.

"Don't worry," he told Juan without accepting the bill back, "the door is below, next to the dining room. There will be someone waiting for you to take you ashore in a dinghy."

"But I — "

"You did what you were supposed to," said Mr. Warrem in a tone that admitted no further discussion, and turning around, he vanished into the circle of his guests.

IT was raining. The kind of aimless and never-ending drizzle, capable of undermining the most cheerful of dispositions. It was the typical gray New York rain, heralding winter, that brings even more chill to our tropical souls than to our bones; the kind that fills us with nostalgia for warm, torrential showers that make the grass smell fresh and the earth glisten and come alive.

Decorating the Christmas tree in the middle of the lobby, our doorman would stop once in a while to go to the big glass door and watch the rain. He did this mechanically, convinced that the pitter patter would not change pace, not a single raindrop more, and not a single raindrop less, for days, for weeks, even months.

Yes, the rain would continue. It would not stop to let in a single bright, sunny day. It would bring instead some dirty snow, which like a grimy crust would stick to the sidewalks, the rooftops, the bare trees, and even to the skin of the unfortunate pedestrians who had no choice but to venture out in such weather.

Juan resumed his task. Now on top of the ladder, he was trimming the cut-down fir tree with bright-colored Christmas balls. Every few minutes he would come down, not only to look at the rain but also to open the door for the tenants returning home with their pets. As soon as they were inside, the animals would shake themselves off, spattering mud and water all over the floor. . . . Fortunately, the person now beckoning at the door was Miss Scarlett Reynolds, whose rag dog at least could not shake itself off. Though it was true this animal did not cause him any inconvenience, the doorman did have to suffer the endless chatter of its mistress. Now retired, she had been a very popular film actress in her time. Who could forget *Pajamas in the Night*, or *Moonbeam on My Heart*? These movies made her both famous and wealthy. But the more money she accumulated, the more miserly she became, to the point that in order to add to her fortune she would refuse to spend money on food. She became so emaciated and shapeless that RKO and other prominent studios finally stopped offering her movie roles, preferring instead simply to pay her the astronomical figures demanded by her contracts.

Miss Reynolds seemed annoyed today, and was coming back from her brief walk at a fantastic speed, considering her fragile condition. Our doorman, after opening the door presto for her, inquired about the reason for her sudden return.

"A housefly on my shoulder tried to steal a free ride. I scared it away, and it landed on my hat and then on my dog. As you will surely understand, I could not allow it to use us for free transportation."

"Of course not," our doorman agreed.

"Oh, by the way," said Miss Reynolds taking off her hat, "could you lend me a dollar? I want to give it to the super to see if he will turn up the heat."

Our doorman handed her a dollar bill, as usual in the hope of engaging her in a deeper kind of conversation, one that would lead to his favorite topic, or rather (it hardly needs to be said) to the only theme he considered important: that famous "true door," which he wanted to open for the poor little rich woman obsessed with frugality.

Right then another tenant was approaching the glass door, and Juan for a moment had to give up his magic door to open the real one. This time it was one of the two Oscars, a rather chubby fellow with fine, arched eyebrows and a haircut so short his head seemed almost shaved. He entered with his bulldog and with the terrified white rabbit, dyed lavender, prudently trailing behind for fear of losing its life at the hands (or in the fangs) of the larger beast. Juan opened the door for them and bowed before climbing the ladder again, trying to resume his conversation with Miss Reynolds. While up in that position, the doorman was being ogled by Oscar (rather, by Oscar One, not to be confused with the other Oscar still upstairs in their apartment). Patronizing as usual, he spoke to Juan while keeping the dog and the rabbit in check. The lighting fixture was not working properly in the kitchen, he said, and would the doorman please (and this sounded more like an order) come up and take a look at it? Our doorman quickly consented and then tried to return to Miss Reynolds and his eternal theme, that cherished door.

But it was not doors, much less imaginary or metaphysical doors, that interested Miss Scarlett Reynolds that afternoon. She wanted to discuss, of course, the high cost of living, and how even the subways were now only for millionaires; how no one who did not have a fortune could dream of going to the movies anymore; and how only the very wealthy could afford to eat or even bathe. Poor little old lady . . .

"Of course," our doorman dared to interject, as he placed another gigantic Christmas ball on the tree, "the problem is, nobody has realized that the most important thing is to find the Great Door. . . ."

"What?" cried Miss Reynolds in astonishment. "Are you telling me they want to change the door now, too? It's ridiculous! Every day they bring something in, take something out, change things around, or simply demolish them. Isn't the door big enough for everybody? And who pays for it? We do, of course!"

"No, no, I'm referring to another door."

"Another door! Why on earth do we need another door? Don't we have enough with this one and the back door, for the thieves to come in and cart away all our possessions? Look, if this goes on, I'll have to sell my apartment and live under a bridge. Yes, under a bridge, like my friend René, Renecito Cifuentes, who was the owner of the famous Cifuentes Cigars and now is totally ruined, like me."

The doorman tried once again to explain to Miss Reynolds what kind of door he was referring to, but she was already convinced that the single purpose of the building management was to make as many "repairs" and "improvements" as possible and have the tenants foot the bills. She became so upset that for a moment she stopped talking, and, dragging the rag dog, she began to nervously pace the lobby. If the weather weren't so cold, the most practical thing to do, as she had been thinking for some time, would be to sell everything and go live on the streets. . . .

Miss Reynolds had already spoken with many homeless people and had come to the conclusion they were the only ones in this country who did not have to waste money on taxes, rent, water bills, electricity, and quite often, even transportation. So she saw herself, perfectly happy, with her rag dog and a shopping bag with all her fortune in it, sleeping under a bridge, perhaps next to Renecito Cifuentes, or in any other forgotten corner of Manhattan. Besides, she had come to know by heart all of the city's sewers, drains, and tunnels since her daily "occupation" consisted of fishing for coins from these underground mazes. With that purpose in mind, she got up every day at dawn and, equipped with a small flashlight, a fishhook, a magnetized sinker, and a long string, she roamed the city. The job was not really complicated, though it's true at times she would get in the way of traffic, or someone would kick her, or a police officer would reproach her. Armed with her flashlight, Miss Reynolds would crouch until she spotted a coin through the grating of the curbside drain, cast down her magnetized sinker, and as soon as it picked up the coin, she would skillfully pull the string, bringing up a penny, a quarter — and even an occasional silver dollar — while the hurried pedestrians eyed her with envy. Sometimes, presuming that the elderly lady had lost her keys or some piece of jewelry, a gentleman would volunteer to help, an offer she would reject crossly, always suspecting a *concealed* motive: sharing of the profits. Anyway, her "fishing" brought in more than enough to cover her expenses, which were minimal, considering that her dog did not eat; that to light her apartment she used candles (made from pieces of soap she picked up in public restrooms); and that she generally managed to eat in soup kitchens around the city.

Miss Reynolds also collected empty cans, bottles, cardboard boxes, and all sorts of plastic containers, all of which had turned her apartment into a veritable junkyard, and which she packed up now and then (with the doorman's help) to exchange for money at the nearest supermarket.

When fishing for coins did not bring in enough, Scarlett Reynolds would beg on the streets. This was profitable indeed, thanks to her apparent advanced age and her crooked, withered figure. We have written "apparent advanced age" because Miss Reynolds was not really as old as she appeared to be. At first glance, it could be said she was in her eighties, but we know for sure she was no more than fifty-five years old. In order to collect for "disability" and avoid paying taxes, she had undergone reverse cosmetic surgery to have her look prematurely like an old lady. And also, though we have no witnesses, it has been said that she once hurled herself under a de luxe limousine so that she could sue the owner, another millionaire like herself who lived in the same neighborhood. . . . Anyway, this aged and deformed figure always inspired a certain pity. For instance, when she accosted our doorman once more to ask for a quarter, Juan, who was covering the fir tree with silvery angels, handed her a dollar, the last one he had in his pocket. Miss Reynolds, as usual, did not thank him and just tucked the bill in the handbag she always carried with her, securely tied to her arm.

"And please don't mention doors again," she told the doorman as she walked away. "Tomorrow morning I will speak to the management and I'll tell them not to count on me. If I have to move from here, then I will!" she blurted finally, thinking perhaps about that bridge that was waiting for her.

Juan made another attempt to explain to her the kind of door he was talking about, but at that moment another egg flashed across the hallway like a comet and smashed into his face.

"It's incredible how people throw money away," was her comment, looking at the egg dripping off the doorman's face. "I hope at least it was rotten."

And with a recriminating look, as if the doorman were responsible for the incident, she walked off, dragging her dog behind her.

· 14 ·

ANNOYED by this new assault, no doubt carried out by Pascal Junior or Nena, his sister, Juan wiped his face and made up his mind this time to go and complain right away to the children's father, Pascal Pietri, the building super. It was dinnertime and he could leave his post. But then he remembered he had something to fix in the Oscars' kitchen, and as the administration never tired of saying, the tenants came first, so he decided to postpone his complaint and his dinner as well.

When the doorman rang the bell, the two Oscars were right at the door, as if they had been standing behind it, waiting for him. Oscar One stepped forward, wrapped in a robe the same shade of lavender as the rabbit. From this evidence the doorman concluded that Oscar One had used the same dye for more than one purpose. Oscar Two greeted Juan in a crimson robe and asked him if he would like something to drink. The doorman excused himself saying he had no time and would prefer to quickly fix whatever needed to be fixed in the kitchen. Then Oscar One made a quick pirouette, took a stepladder out of a closet, and placed it under the kitchen lamp. The doorman, who already had the proper tools, started his electrician's job while, standing next to the ladder, the two Oscars watched him approvingly and winked at each other in secret understanding.

We consider it indispensable for the accuracy of this true story to introduce these two characters, the two Oscars, more fully. For one thing, only one of them was American. The other, Oscar One, was a Cuban who had come to the United States with the Mariel exodus in 1980. Upon his arrival in New York, Ramón García Pérez (which is his real name) met John Scott, which is Oscar Two's real name. The truth is, Ramón García had never wanted to be Ramón García but rather some famous Hollywood star with an exotic yet Anglo-Saxon name. Mr. Scott was not happy with his name either, since both his first and last names reminded him too much of his early family life on an Ohio farm. Ramón and John moved in together, not because they were lovers (each really preferred a different type), but because they pursued similar types: tough, low-class men, hoodlums, aspiring gangsters. And to help matters along, Oscar Two's father, rejecting his gay son, decided to give him a large sum of money on condition he would never ever hear from him again.

The pursuit commonly shared by Oscar One and Oscar Two had never come to fruition, except of course that they changed their names to Oscar, with the same last name, Times. The idea for both to take the same name came from Ramón García, who, right after leaving his country, had promised himself in a burst of frivolity and justified resentment: first, never again to speak a word in Spanish; and second, to assimilate in his adopted country to such a degree that no one could ever guess he had been born in a remote Cuban town to the south of the province of Santa Clara, called Muelas Quietas (Quiet Jaws).

Ramón García was very superficial and a real snob. He started by finding a new first and last name for himself that would symbolize what he considered to be the supreme icons of his new country: the Hollywood Oscar and *The New York Times*.

During the ten years Mr. García (or rather, Mr. Times) has lived in New York, he has seen every Oscar-nominated movie at least a dozen times. If you take into account that Oscar nominations range from best cinematography to best song, you can imagine the amount of time he has wasted in those ten years. And regarding *The New York Times*, his passion for this newspaper is such that since his arrival he has bought, and saved, every single issue; the large apartment where he lives is a mountain of papers that covers all the wall area from floor to ceiling, a disaster about to happen. Ramón García's blind fanaticism fascinated John Scott, who basically felt flattered to think that this exotically tropical, provincial, misshapen human being was desperately trying, after all, to be like him, John Scott, the perfect model (which is how he saw himself) of a young, good-looking, gay American male. Therefore, John welcomed enthusiastically the idea of changing his name as well. And so, precisely because of his powerful obsession with becoming a "typical American gay," Ramón García (and how he loathed this name) actually managed to surpass his model, thus becoming Oscar Times One, not Oscar Times Two, in the new name register. Both Oscars nevertheless remained nothing like the physical image they had of themselves. Instead of young, athletic, attractive men, they were two effeminate beings, bald and fat, who sat every morning with their toast and decaffeinated coffee, reading *The New York Times*.... After which, with an identical walk and dressed in the same style (following the latest fashion set by some Hollywood idol), they would go out cruising in search of the ideal lover, a man who, of course, was nowhere to be found. In the course of their many outings they had explored public restrooms and rooftops, stairways and trains, beaches, jailhouses and movie houses, bars, military bases, sports stadiums, Turkish baths, museums, and bus stops, naturally not forgetting every tree, archway, bridge, and gazebo in Central Park. They had even roamed the same Bronx Zoo where Mary Avilés has longed for the improbable good fortune of someday being cut to pieces by one of the wild beasts.... Well past midnight, dressed as men but hoping to be raped by some macho man, they had strolled through the center of Harlem all the way uptown; dressed in drag, and hoping to attract some lively transvestite on the make, they had combed every gay hangout, from an underground den called La Escuelita (The Little Schoolhouse) to the crowded sidewalks of 42nd Street.

Of course we are not going to claim that through all this incessant cruising the Oscars never found partners. On the contrary, they found them every day, or rather, day and night; but instead of their passionately desired ideal lovers, they picked up people like themselves, a set of characters they actually despised — rather than desired — and who, in turn, despised them. Only out of boredom, frustration, habit, or just as the last resort did they end up sleeping together, but at the moment of reaching climax, instead of pleasure they experienced the frustration of possessing or being possessed by repulsive mirror images of themselves.

And yet, those were the good times. What came later was much worse. The traditional risks of the easy pickup (blackmail, beatings, theft, venereal disease) changed to a veritable death threat. Of course we are referring to AIDS, the plague of modern times that has taken the lives of 4,200,033 people so far — these are our figures, so they are correct. Until the years 1984–1985 the two Oscars at least were able to put their energy into their search, but now they could no longer do that. During the last five years, growing more desperate every day while appearing serene, they had been experimenting with every kind of sexual aid and equipment, from plastic dildos to aluminum vibrators, including of course the famous Erotic Robot, which has earned billions for its Japanese inventors. But none of these articles brought them — satisfaction's not the word — even relief. Moreover, even though they avidly read *The New York Times* every day, they could find no other solution to their dilemma.

It was then that the two Oscars had their palms read by a witch named Lola Prida, for $500 apiece. She had also escaped Cuba on the Mariel boat lift and had successfully opened a *botánica* (a folk-religious medicinal-herb store) in Queens. She had recommended, and then helped them to acquire, the bulldog and the rabbit.

This is what these animals did for them, after some rudimentary training by Lola: one of the Oscars would undress and lie face down on a mattress made of hundreds of copies of *The New York Times*. While holding the rabbit at the end of a leash, the other Oscar would sic the bulldog on the rodent, which was kept on the other side of the stretched-out Oscar, and the dog, lunging for the creature, would stumble upon the naked body. The standing Oscar then would pull the leash and bring the rabbit in closer. When the bulldog seemed on the verge of devouring the rabbit, his owner would play out enough leash so that, unable to reach the persecuted animal, the enormous dog would bite the reclining Oscar instead. With skill and after weeks of practice, each Oscar Times managed to have the dog unerringly sink its teeth deeply into the other Oscar's buttocks. On occasion this ritual reached blood-curdling proportions. It was pandemonium: the rabbit squealing desperately, the bulldog barking louder and louder in an angry crescendo, and the horizontal Oscar Times letting out peals of pleasure — and of pain, naturally. By the time it was the other Oscar's turn, the apartment reverberated like a wild jungle, while the blood splattered and flowed over the endless stacks of old *New York Times*.

This kind of ceremony seemed to appease the two Oscars. Besides, they developed a growing affection for the dog and the rabbit, and taking them out for a walk, all dressed up in their outlandish garb, was also part of the fun. But it boiled down to a brief consolation: the dissatisfaction and desperation in these matched, misshapen bodies kept increasing ... to the point where they added yet another ritual to their daily routine: when they got up in the morning, after dutifully responding to the call of nature, each would shove an empty Perrier bottle (small size) up his ass — that was why they both walked around with such tight buttocks. But this sexual trick did not put an end to their restlessness; instead it got worse.

For this reason, when Oscar Times One looked closely at our doorman's physical attributes, the thought came to him that this young man could really be the solution to all those painful years of searching. As the two Oscars stood around the stepladder — on top of which Juan was trying to keep his balance, they were thinking what a fine specimen he was, truly masculine, and at the same time an affable and earnest fellow. And, best of all, he was not yet contaminated by greed the way, without a doubt, most young men were in New York, especially the most sought-after hustlers, who, naturally, were the most attractive. Our doorman was their main *objective* now, their star of salvation. He had finished his task, by the way, and was about to come down the ladder and leave.

But then the two Oscars led Juan to the living room. Putting aside some hundred editions of *The New York Times*, they made room on the sofa and sat next to him. Oscar Two offered him a Coke while Oscar One brought some cream cheese and crackers. Oscar Two stuffed a $10 bill into Juan's jacket pocket and Oscar One gave him a fake-silver cigarette lighter. Oscar Two mixed whiskey and orange juice for him. Then Oscar One rushed to open a bottle of champagne, while Oscar Two began dancing to disco music, his robe wide open.

What we might call the crucial stage of the takeover was carried out by Oscar One when, with the pretext that after such an "exhausting" job, our doorman ought to be "dead," he slipped off Juan's shoes for him. Oscar Two did not let Oscar One get too far ahead of him, and still leaning on the columns of *The New York Times*, he knelt before the doorman and started to unzip Juan's pants.

Our doorman, meanwhile, did not know what to do. Should he leave and thus lose his opportunity to lure these unfortunate beings into the search for the mysterious Great Door? Or should he stay and risk being raped by the Oscars while trying to *convert* them? And, on the other hand, didn't he feel the voluptuous pleasure that almost every man experiences when someone, it doesn't matter who, is caressing his testicles? . . . Naturally, though we sympathize with human weaknesses, we must strongly condemn the attitudes and activities indulged in by the two Oscars, and we also repudiate our doorman's moral vacillation. However, we are sure that, in Juan's case, what seduced him to stay, more than pleasure, was his sense of duty as a zealous proselytizer combined with the fear that these tenants might be offended if he rejected their advances, and that their complaints might lead to his dismissal. . . . Anyway, by now the two Oscars together, to the rhythm of that infernal music, had succeeded in lowering the doorman's pants and were desperately trying to arouse him with the skillful play of their tongues.

At this point, with his pants down to his ankles and his shirt open, the doorman spoke.

"And you, don't you have another door?"

"No. Don't worry," Oscar One assured him in his perfectly accented English, "the only door to the outside is locked," and he dived again between Juan's legs.

"It is always good to think about *other doors*," said th· doorman, as if talking to himself.

"You don't need any more doors here. Anyway, there is no danger. We have an excellent doorman," Oscar Two said, going back to his careful inspection.

Things were going very well for the two Oscars. The doorman was already excited, and as if this weren't enough, while they were kissing his member, he was promising to take them to "places where they would feel better than ever before" (naturally, they misunderstood Juan's meaning) and where he was going "*to open* to them" — in their enthusiasm that verb was all they heard — "a way, other ways . . . ," which for them could only mean ways of achieving sexual pleasure, and they were becoming more and more excited.

"Yes! Yes!" the two Oscars cried, thinking that they had finally found what they had been desperately and dangerously looking for: *a real man, un hombre,* a true man who not only would pleasure them, but who also offered them manly protection and even a solid future, in every sense of the word. . . .

Now they were reaching the last stage of the ceremony, the coupling. The two Oscars sprang to their feet, turning extremely nimble, weightless even, in spite of their enormous size. Overcome by a euphoria such as they had never experienced before, they started to dance in anticipation to the pulsing beat of a Michael Jackson tape that was now thundering through the speakers.

In homage to the doorman, the two Oscars, now completely

naked, were jumping all around the pages of *The New York Times*. They joined hands, and bumped against each other's belly; they bowed so deeply their bald spots touched. Finally they backed up to the stacks of newspapers rising vertically against the walls, and back to back they met again, smacking each other's behind as if in a congratulatory greeting before the banquet. . . . But, alas, something totally unforeseen and terrible occurred just then: when they smacked their buttocks together, the empty Perrier bottles they had inserted in their asses — which in the heat of passion they had forgotten to remove — shattered, causing serious, almost fatal injuries to both of them. Once again a bloodbath flowed over the stacks of old newspapers, and laughter turned into shrieks of pain.

Our doorman, coming to his senses, immediately phoned for an ambulance.

The two Oscars were taken immediately to emergency surgery at Roosevelt Hospital, where they both underwent *colostomies*; that is, each had to have an artificial anus inserted on the side of his abdomen. Their malicious friends began to say that their restlessness surely would double. . . . On the other hand, our reliable informants, placed everywhere as you might have guessed, tell us that after this accident they stopped being called Oscar Times by their friends: they were now referred to as "Double Barrels," a name that was indeed a blow to the Timeses' self-respect, and that totally demoralized them.

It was not on our agenda to tell this sad and embarrassing story, but the story of our doorman, which is enough. Now we must go on.

· 15 ·

RIGHT after the ambulance left with the two Oscars, Juan returned to his post properly attired. Once again he had missed his mealtime, and therefore he decided to postpone going to see the super until the next day, to present his complaint. And this is the way things happened.

Juan knew that to visit the super meant again giving up his dinner break. Just to get an answer at the door took more than half an hour, and besides, for him to tell the super about the endless mischief his children had gotten into was of no use since Pietri knew perfectly well what went on and had done nothing about it. What's more, Juan had a suspicion that many of the pranks Pascal Junior and his sister Nena were involved in were directed by the super himself. Obviously, if Pascal Junior threw eggs at Juan's face, it was not only for his own amusement; he was following orders from his father, who was bent on making life impossible for our doorman: he wanted that job for one of his nephews, just arrived from Italy.

Juan was not alone in his predicament. Every tenant in the building was a victim of the super's shady manipulations. Mr. Pietri was constantly shutting off the hot water, or the heat, on the pretense that the "boilah," as he used to say, was broken. However, as soon as the protesting tenant would slip a few dollars into his pocket, the boilah would get fixed as if by magic. To make some extra money (and the truth is his wages were very low) he would cause short circuits, which he then efficiently repaired. He would close the gas valve, and a $20 bill could open it immediately; he would plant mice, cockroaches, and even fire ants throughout the building, and then, under some "bankable" pressure, would exterminate them in a wink. He would also have his kids throw stones to break windows, or stomp on the roof (which in New York was made of cardboard), so that he could, "for a modest sum," make the needed repairs.

Right before he opened the door for Juan, Mr. Pietri had been feeding some voracious rats he planned to let loose in the apartments of some of the wealthier tenants.

The doorman respectfully greeted Mr. Pietri, who, without bothering to answer him or to put down the cage with the rats, motioned him to sit down. But there was no place to sit. The chairs and armchairs, the loveseat, and the sofa (each with bright red upholstery to match the curtains) were cluttered with a variety of objects: plastic flowers, dolls without arms, tattered books, chicken bones, dumbbells, underwear, half-eaten fruits, dirty socks, records and cassettes, dead batteries, and a thousand other things. It was clear that the seats in this house were not reserved for human beings. And above it all floated a haze of dust that made breathing difficult.... Even Mrs. Pietri, on her feet and plucking a chicken in the middle of the dining room, was unable to stop sneezing and occasionally disappeared from view in a cloud of dust. On the table was a collection of empty cans and opened jelly jars, shriveled vegetables, a few rubber balls, some filthy hairbrushes, an enormous tape player turned up to full volume, frying pans, dishes of abandoned food, a wilted houseplant, and even a red umbrella, which Pascal Junior, while he hollered songs, was stripping just as if it were the chicken his mother was working on. The "baby" of the family, Nena, was busy moving around on the floor. She was a red and round little monster of about nine, and looked very much like her father. Between insolent, teasing glances at the doorman, she was now finishing off a dish of grated coconut in heavy syrup with American cheese. This was Mrs. Pietri's national dish, for she was not Italian like her husband, but her maiden name was Belkis Malet and she had been born in Cuba.

Still standing, our doorman looked around and noticed that Pascal Junior was listening to a different beat from that of the tape player on the table. His headphones were connected to a Walkman radio tied to his ample waistline. Juan was stunned to discover that the five little chihuahuas barking and jumping around Mrs. Pietri, no doubt disturbed by the doorman's presence, were also wearing earphones, but these were connected to small cassette players tied around their bellies and blasting away on their own. Their yelping seemed to be a faithful imitation of the music (or rather, the noise) they were hearing. At least that's what Juan thought and jotted down in his diary.

In spite of the racket produced by the dogs and the tape players, plus the ripping sounds coming from the umbrella Pascal Junior was eviscerating, our doorman did try to say a few words. Of course he did not wish to make a direct, personal complaint to Mr. Pascal Pietri about his son, but rather to present the case on behalf of all the tenants and say that, though he was deeply sorry, he had no choice but to pass this information on. After that, he hoped he might be able to bring the conversation around to his personal agenda, and talk about the Great Door.

However, nothing came of his plan. Mr. Pietri was the one who did all the talking, precisely to complain about the doorman's irresponsible behavior, his negligence, and, in general, his very unsatisfactory performance. The carpets in the hallway were dirty, the mirrors in the lobby grimy, the golden doorknobs on the big glass door had no shine, bulbs in the chandelier needed changing ... Our doorman could have argued, of course, that his job was only to open and close the door and to watch for the tenants' safety, but how could he as long as Mr. Pietri's tirade went on and on? To make matters worse, the blaring music and the yelping dogs were driving him crazy. Even Mrs. Pietri, who must have been used to that din, walked toward Pascal Junior holding her half-plucked chicken by the neck, and threatened to hit him on the head with it if he didn't lower the volume on the big noisy machine; though it must be said, Pascal Junior could not even hear the tape player since he was only listening to the radio connected to his earphones. And in any case it was not the music from either one that held Pascal Junior's attention. He was wholly concentrated on destroying the umbrella and was ignoring everything else. Taking advantage of this, Mrs. Pietri, with a single blow, turned off the infernal machine without his noticing. He had already stripped the fabric from the metal ribs and was bending them back and forth until they broke off from the pole. Since this did not seem enough, he crushed each rib, one by one, and finally, jumping up and down on it, he reduced the handle to smithereens. After nothing of the umbrella remained, he turned his attention to a stuffed chair, which he began to disembowel after sweeping off all the junk piled on top of it. At that point the super, still holding the cage full of rats in one hand, ran to a back room where he kept, as he had told the doorman, several tenants' complaints. In the meantime, Mrs. Pietri, still in the middle of the room, eyed the doorman with a stern, mistrustful gaze as if he were, at any moment, about to run away with a lamp, a chair, or any of the other household objects, an action only she could prevent by her obvious display of strict vigilance.

Pascal Junior had now gutted the upholstered chair and, armed with a hammer, was whacking away at what was left (the legs, the back, the rungs) until it all became a heap of firewood. Quite satisfied with his accomplishment, he returned to the radio on the table, turning the volume all the way up. Then, energized by the beat of the music, he took the hammer and hurled it against the wall, shattering the glass frame of a large print that showed outsized pink flamingos resting on one leg, huddled under a flamboyant in full bloom.

"Look what you did to your new clothes! Your new suit is filthy!" Mrs. Pietri ranted, still keeping watch over the doorman.

We must admit that even though Pascal Junior and Nena were twelve and nine, they were always properly attired. Today Pascal was wearing high suede boots, a green gabardine suit with red velveteen vest over a salmon-colored silk shirt, and a little black bow around his neck. Nena was wearing, or showing off, a big pink wool skirt, lavender blouse with flaring sleeves, and bright-colored ribbons and bows on the bodice as well as on her hair and nonexistent waist. Small golden bows covered the tips of her shoes, which had once been white. Both children wore gold jewelry, watches and rings as well as bracelets and chains with dangling silver and gold amulets, and medallions stamped with the images of Nuestra Señora de la Caridad del Cobre (Our Lady of Charity), Cuba's patron saint, and of Our Lady of Loreto. A strong scent permeated their bodies and not very clean outfits. To top it all off, the whole house reeked of a mixture of *sofrito* (garlic, onion, tomato, green pepper, and spices) and bay rum as well as unflushed toilets and room freshener, chlorine bleach and rat urine, talcum powder and sweaty clothes, and dog poop and Chanel No. 5. It seemed that stench and perfume were locked in an incessant battle they took turns at winning.

Juan also noticed that above that jumble of junk, furniture, and blending of dust, colors, and smells, the ceiling seemed to sparkle in a world of its own. Mrs. Pietri had had it enameled and speckled with sequins and golden spangles, remotely resembling a starry sky. Juan was going to say something about a cornucopia of wax tropical fruit displayed on a short plaster pillar when Mr. Pietri returned brandishing a letter of complaint against the doorman, signed by none other than Miss Reynolds, "one of the most respectable ladies in the building," the super quickly added. "What did she complain about?" our doorman wanted to know. The voice of the super soon rose above the uproar, and even dominated the blaring music.

Miss Reynolds had complained that the doorman was not careful enough with the tenants' property, that he even tried to destroy it, obviously intending to make a profit on the repairs. And the letter went on, complaining that the doorman had even suggested replacing the front door. " 'He will surely have something to gain from this scheme,' " Miss Reynolds's letter rattled on. " 'For a few dollars' profit, I am sure he is perfectly willing to break the door himself. But I am not willing to allow him, or anyone else, to pilfer away my money. Either you fire him or I'll sell my apartment and move out. . . .' "

Juan could not believe his ears, but before he could protest, the super put away the threatening letter and pulled out another sheet. This one, signed by Brenda Hill, complained that he had proposed to knock down a wall in her apartment " 'in order to build me another door.' " She added that thanks only to her extreme patience and good manners she " 'had been able to dissuade him from his insane project, all the more since the wall in question connects with Mr. Lockpez's apartment. . . .' "

"And right here I also have a complaint from Mr. Lockpez. He says you refuse to pay attention to his 'spiritual and moral guidance,' and that you are 'extremely absent-minded in the performance of your important duties regarding security and maintenance of —' " The super stopped reading as if he had given enough from Mr. Lockpez and, abandoning his ironic tone for a more serious one, started to read another complaint, this one signed by Dr. Joseph Rozeman the eminent dentist, who contended, he said, that " 'quite often the doorman has a sickening bad breath, smelling of rotten eggs. . . .' "

"It's precisely about the rotten eggs that I came to see you," Juan managed to get in. But then the super, finally dropping the caged rats on the floor, and raising in both hands a letter with an ostentatious letterhead, thundered: "And this is really serious! A complaint from Mr. Warrem!" And at the mention of the magnate's name, Mrs. Pietri stopped plucking the chicken, Nena stopped gulping a chocolate pie, and even Pascal Junior turned down his tape machine. "Mr. Warrem himself," Pascal Pietri raved on, "complained that you have overstepped your position as doorman and tried to be too familiar with his regal pet, Cleopatra." For a few moments they all stared in shock and disbelief at Juan, who, completely devastated, lowered his eyes. "I never imagined you could be so reckless," cried the super. "Mr. Warrem is practically the owner of this building! And by the way, he complains too that you smell. . . . And here is another grievance from Miss Reynolds, where she says, 'the doorman has dared to pet my dog with his dirty hands.' " And here

Mr. Pietri looked at the doorman and commented sarcastically, "It seems you have a thing for dogs."

Then, pulling out another piece of paper, he continued: "Ah, this is also a very serious complaint. It's signed by Mrs. Levinson. She calls you 'rude and impolite,' and 'not suited to hold a position as important as that of doorman, which requires social awareness and tact.' She also accuses you of 'un-cons-cio-nable immaturity' " (and Mr. Pietri had some trouble pronouncing the word). "So you have also been disrespectful to Mrs. Levinson! Didn't you know she is a lawyer and she can send you to jail? . . . Of course," the super added in a condescending tone, "I can't go on and on, I have many things to do!" He meant it was time for Juan to leave. "Unless you shape up, you know what will happen to you!"

The doorman tried to think of something to say, perhaps to promise he would be more careful in the future, but he felt so confused and humiliated by all those letters he did not know what to think. Anyway, he opened his mouth to say something, but the cloud of dust swirling inside the house forced him to sneeze instead.

"I see you have nothing to say," cried Mr. Pietri triumphantly.

And when Juan sneezed for the second time, Mrs. Pietri glanced at him with such disapproval that our doorman thought that if he did not leave immediately, that woman was going to hit him with the chicken she had just finished plucking.

Already standing at the door, the super now dismissed him explosively.

"And don't bother me anymore if it isn't something really important. Oh, and as far as *those doors* you want to make, don't you forget that around here I am the only carpenter!"

16

IN total despair, Juan returned to his post by the door. Of course he didn't think he had any right to ask the tenants to explain any of their complaints, even though he was completely sure that most of them were unfair. He continued to open the door for them in his usual courteous manner, fearing that if he greeted them in a more laconic way, he might appear either disrespectful or moody, something a doorman should not do. Even when Miss Reynolds asked him for three dollars instead of the habitual quarter or dollar, our doorman handed her a $5 bill (all he had) and smiled with apprehension: Would Miss Reynolds be offended by his giving her more than she had asked?

The last tenant to return was Dr. Joseph Rozeman, with his three lady-dogs flaunting their perfect, pearly white teeth. They all joined their master in greeting the doorman with big, bright, matching smiles. Recalling Dr. Rozeman's complaint about his bad breath, Juan tried not to open his mouth too wide as he smiled back at the eminent dentist, for he could not be really sure Dr. Rozeman's complaint was unfounded. We can reassure you it was, since our doorman seldom had bad breath. Dr. Rozeman had made that complaint strictly for business reasons. Some time ago he had suggested that Juan have all his teeth pulled and replaced with a permanent prosthesis, a special denture of his own invention cast in silver and porcelain, which would look "so much better than your own teeth," as Dr. Rozeman, also renowned as a dental engineer, had said to

Juan. But since the doorman had hesitated to agree to the unaffordable $5,000 fee, Dr. Rozeman, with an extra prosthesis on hand created especially for him (as we shall see), was pressuring and conspiring with the super to persuade Juan to accept his services.

As Dr. Rozeman said goodbye to the young man with what he considered an elegant gesture, and flashed his wide smile with long, even teeth, he looked at Juan earnestly and announced that he would be working in his laboratory until dawn and that, if Juan so desired, he could stop by for a visit and have the honor of seeing his "special creations."

It was an invitation our doorman could not possibly refuse.

Shortly after midnight, Juan rang the bell at the apartment. Dr. Rozeman himself opened the door and led him to his *laboratory*. It was an enormous workshop for the manufacture of every kind of denture imaginable.

Dr. Rozeman grabbed the doorman by the arm and began his guided tour around the shop, showing him the life-size casts of the people for whom he had engineered what he called "The Smile of Happiness."

While they walked, the doctor carried a metal case. From it, as he approached each of the casts, he would take out a numbered set of dentures, put them in place, and thus transform the mannequin so miraculously that it could easily be mistaken for a live person. We should add that these figures were dressed in the same style of clothes worn by their real counterparts, sometimes even with such accuracy and grace that, once the prostheses were set in place, they looked more authentic than their models. . . . By the way, before going on with this true story, we should say that many members of our prosperous Cuban community have availed themselves of Dr. Rozeman's services with such success that some have come to be presidents of international banks, heads of railroad lines, chancellors of state universities, mayors of U.S. cities, and even ambassadors to key nations in the world. All of these people had followed Dr. Rozeman's wise counsel: "A beautiful smile can save not only your future but the future of all humanity as well." As an even greater attraction for his prospective patients, Dr. Rozeman had in his studio replicas of some of the big personalities or celebrities for whom he had created "a smile for eternity." And all these stars — with their two sets of dentures, the one they wore and the other a spare that the foresighted dentist kept always ready for them in case of an accident — would light up the workshop with their gleaming smiles of porcelain or pearl, depending on the client's resources.

Led by the strong arm of the aging dentist, who was, of course, a very wealthy man, our doorman could contemplate in awe the secret behind the fixed expression of happiness that has always brightened Maria Schell's face; the large, defiant, and sensual teeth of Sophia Loren; the seductive, even bite of Ingrid Bergman (Dr. Rozeman's first great triumph); he could also admire the slightly irregular teeth, for greater authenticity, of Rock Hudson; the tiny rodentlike teeth (crucial to his public success) of Ed Koch, ex-Mayor of New York; and Ronald Reagan's unflappable, frozen smile of triumph, a smile that even his death two years ago was not able to erase from his mummified face. . . . For truth's sake it is necessary to point out that Dr. Rozeman did have professional ethics, and at times, even when he was offered huge sums, he would refuse to make a permanent prosthesis for someone whose facial features he considered unworthy of his talents, when the ugliness was so pervasive that even the most beautiful pearly teeth could do nothing for it. That was precisely the case with Geraldine Champlain. Sometimes, despite the astronomical sum offered him, Dr. Rozeman declined it repeatedly, pleading an overload of back orders, while saying to himself that on such a homely face his work would lose all its merit and could even damage his solid reputation.

Nonetheless, as a tireless inventor, the prominent dental engineer had also specialized in fashioning permanent dentures for the pets of those wealthy enough to afford them. So Juan found out that Brenda Hill's cat possessed brilliant porcelain teeth that had cost her owner fifteen thousand dollars.

Also a few of Mr. Lockpez's parrots had ceramic beaks, and even Cassandra Levinson's bear (and here was the replica) had a set of canines made of coral, the kinds of polyps Miss Levinson had grown fond of after reading that Pablo Neruda, the famous Marxist poet, collected them, along with other souvenirs from the sea. Later Dr. Rozeman also showed Juan a sculptured copy of Mr. Makadam's orangutan, whose apparently ferocious platinum teeth had blunted tips.

"At least," said Dr. Rozeman then, "if the animal runs around loose, he won't be able to do much harm. . . ."

After having seen those special incisors, a bit larger than the natural ones, it wasn't difficult for Juan to understand why Dr. Rozeman's dogs always seemed to be smiling; the large, permanent crowns implanted by their master forced them to show their teeth all the time.

But if this whole demonstration of dentures and cast figures had astonished Juan, the biggest surprise came when Dr. Rozeman with great flourish released the doorman's elbow and, stepping toward a compartment, swept aside a black curtain to reveal Juan's own double!

Our doorman found himself suddenly facing his own image, wearing his own uniform, with exactly the same hat and gloves, exactly the same hair style and appearance, except that the smile was so triumphal, and therefore so dehumanized, that the real-life doorman was sharply taken aback, staring in awe at his own image but unable to identify himself fully with his replica. He felt devastated when Dr. Rozeman turned an intense spotlight on the model and began to speak.

"By changing only your teeth, you can insure your future." Dr. Rozeman's logic made complete sense. That doorman who smiled at our doorman seemed blissfully ignorant of life's tribulations and even more unconcerned about finding some special, mysterious door for every tenant in his building. Far removed from all that, the other Juan, whose smile exuded confidence and masculine self-assertiveness, was evidently not a doorman who would have to open or search for doors: he was a man for whom all doors would open instantly. Facing his double, the real Juan felt like his own doorman. And while Dr. Rozeman urged Juan to have his teeth removed and be transformed to look like that triumphant mannequin, our doorman understood that by so doing, he, the true doorman, would disappear forever, along with his unusual, but for him extraordinary, mission.

"I can truly understand," Dr. Rozeman was saying, sure that he had gained a new patient, "how impressed you must be. You had no idea how perfect a job I could do for you. And don't worry, for you alone, I am going to make it a really low price: after all, as a doorman you'll be great advertising for me. If you wish" — and now his tone had become familiar — "we can start right now taking out those teeth in order to give you the smile of success."

But then, for the first time in his many months as a doorman, Juan declined out loud the suggestions of one of his employers. "No!" he shouted.

A mere monosyllable, but so desperate and resolute it stunned Dr. Rozeman to realize — for the first time in his entire professional career — that he was losing a patient he thought already in his grasp. But as a businessman, and thus a diplomat to the end, he tried once more to convince the doorman. "You can arrange for easy payments," he said, displaying his own beautiful teeth made of cultured pearls.

But it was useless: uttering another piercing NO, the doorman ran as fast as he could across the workshop; he was feeling persecuted and almost trapped, not only by Dr. Rozeman's triumphant smile but also by those of all the personalities, including the animals and — above all — by the smile from his own double, ordering him to return and put himself in the hands of the eminent specialist. In a panic, he reached the door, which he furiously slammed back in the faces of Dr. Rozeman's three lady-dogs, almost hitting their resplendent dentures. Then (though we are sure this couldn't really have happened) our doorman thought that the smiles of all those mannequins, including his own, turned into a roar of mocking laughter resounding through the entire building.

17

A N almost bottomless despair took hold of our doorman after the encounter with the super and his visit with Dr. Rozeman. As if these weren't enough troubles, about the same time the Doormen's Union of New York passed a resolution, in response to the many complaints lodged by tenants and guests, which forbade doormen to watch television, read, write, or listen to the radio during working hours. Juan wasn't interested in either radio or television, but he did like to read in his free moments, and especially (and this was more a necessity than a diversion) to make notes, his duties permitting, in the notebook he kept, as we have said, in his jacket — a notebook that has helped us a great deal in this report. . . . When he first saw the bulletin listing the prohibitions, the doorman thought it was the super's new way of harassing him, but it was easy for him to confirm that the document was authentic and had to be strictly observed — a practical impossibility for Juan because, in his view, the notes he kept on the tenants and of his own thoughts (also jotted down) were like records and signs he believed would light the way to the door of redemption. Without these notes (that is what he wrote, despite the prohibition) how was he going to discover and study the true personalities of his protégés (yes, "protégés" is what he wrote), the ones he was responsible for saving (and yes, "saving" is the word he used)? How then could he help them? And if he couldn't help them, how was he to go on living?

So, despite the union's resolution, our doorman continued to write down his observations, now more surreptitiously, while at the same time treating all the tenants more graciously than ever.

Precisely to ingratiate himself further and to take advantage of the Christmas spirit, Juan thought it would be best to give the tenants presents, especially to those who had lodged complaints about his services. Though tradition dictated that it was the doorman who should receive tips or Christmas gifts from the tenants, in this case he considered it his duty to give something to them.

In all fairness, however, one must admit that nearly all the tenants, including those who had faulted his job performance, gave our doorman some kind of gift. Some, like Mr. Warrem, had handed him an envelope with $200; others gave him only a dollar, and as incredible as it may seem, even Miss Reynolds, instead of asking our doorman for money, had with great ceremony handed him a quarter, preceded by a little lecture that simply must be included.

"We all know, my dear friend, that the Management has given you the Christmas bonus you are entitled to, but I personally want to contribute to their funds, which are much more solid than mine. I hope you know how to appreciate the value of this gift and the sacrifice it means for me. I hope you don't waste it, but use it as an incentive to save a little more, day by day. Deposit it in a savings account, and many years from now you will want to thank me for it."

And so, with all that money — $2,115.25 — our doorman went along to the famous *Nancy's* department store to buy the gifts that he intended to give the tenants.

Upon entering the enormous building (some say it is the largest store in the world),* and before Juan had a chance to

---

* We want to record in this document that the important retail establishment Nancy's is owned by a Cuban lady, Nancy E. Añeja, who began her mercantile endeavors fifty years ago selling used books in Hialeah, Florida; and thanks to her determination and enterprising spirit, she is today one of the wealthiest women in the country. For more on this subject read the remarkable study *Women at the Top* by Ismael Lorenzo, published by SIBE, Miami, 1989.

even think about what to choose, several elegantly dressed salesladies took both his hands and scented them with eleven kinds of different lotions and colognes. Our doorman, who had never been there before, thought that he had come to the wrong place, but the salesladies quickly made him understand that these were simply free samples of perfume so that he might select the one he liked best. He really was planning to buy one or another, thinking it would make an appropriate gift; but by now the elegant salesladies had completely forgotten him and, still smiling, were perfuming another man.

Juan started to move on, but just then a woman wearing a raincoat and carrying a watering can stepped up to him and, without further ado, slipped a raincoat on him — similar to the one she was wearing — and, before he could say a word, emptied the can over his head, thus demonstrating the effectiveness of the article he had on, which Nancy's was now offering at a special price. Our doorman, his hair soaked, thanked the saleslady and thought to himself that buying raincoats for the tenants was also a good idea, for if there's anything one always needs in New York, it's a raincoat. But two very friendly men in uniform were already removing the raincoat while the saleslady with the watering can sprinkled another gentleman, and so Juan took the escalator going up.

On the second floor, two young ladies in nightgowns made him sit on a large sofa and, since our doorman didn't object, they had him lie down on the couch, which instantly converted into a bed. While one of the employees began enumerating all the wonderful features of this piece, the other one, by adjusting the mattress, was trying to rock the potential buyer like a baby. Listening to the sales pitch, and letting himself be rocked blissfully, Juan nodded politely after each point, so that when it ended a third saleslady had already filled out his bill of sale for the sofa bed at, she said, a give-away "family price" — only $3,500 down and $300 a month for three years. Truly embarrassed, our doorman explained that his money wouldn't go that far; he began making other excuses, but by then Juan seemed to have become suddenly invisible: the young ladies ignored him completely and were busy with an elderly matron, whom they had already managed to seat on the extravagant piece of furniture. Somewhat relieved, our doorman went up to the very noisy third floor. A split second later, prodded by the pleas of an effective salesman, he found himself operating pressure cookers, electric teakettles, humidifiers, lawn mowers, washing machines, a giant-screen TV monitor, and even a sophisticated portable robot that could do all sorts of domestic jobs, from answering the phone to washing dishes. Finally, the salesman placed in his hands an enormous vacuum cleaner so powerful that when our doorman tried to handle it, having pressed the top-speed button, it dragged him clear across the huge sales floor till it crashed into the elevator door, which was just starting to open. Releasing the vacuum cleaner, Juan got in the elevator and went up to the fifth floor.

Though it was snowing heavily outside, everything on display here was for summer. Beautiful bikini-clad models strolled around in a 90-degree atmosphere. Our doorman was now practically naked beneath a powerful tanning lamp; while he enjoyed skilled hands anointing him with a suntan lotion, our doorman could not avoid hearing the litany of its virtues. "No other lotion combines so many special emollients fortified with a triple natural vitamin," explained the completely dry bathing beauty beneath the shimmering beach umbrella.... But for him to show up on December 31 with bottles of tanning lotion as presents — well, even to our half-dressed doorman, that seemed a bit preposterous, and he decided to escape to the top floor.

As the elevator door opened, a football struck his head. Juan thought the toss had been accidental, but then another ball pounded his stomach, and seeing a third one approaching, he caught it before it could strike. The employee who was throwing the shots clapped with joy and began praising Juan's excellent athletic skills, while continuing to throw one ball after another — each one being, according to the salesman, "the top quality there is on the market." But as Juan was catching and knocking down balls, it occurred to him that a sports ball wasn't a very appropriate gift for people of a certain age, so he rejected the offer. Then the same clerk (or was it another in identical uniform?) very skillfully slipped on his hands a pair of boxing gloves and, before our doorman could protest, began punching him with pretty professional jabs. Juan had to counter with some punches of his own while a voice carried on about the special features of the gloves.

Trying to defend himself, Juan didn't realize he was backing onto a terrace that was also crowded with sporting equipment. A heavyset lady there, dressed entirely in green, awaited him, holding a parachute. None other than Nancy Añeja, always eager to set an example, had taken on the responsibility of selling the most outlandish articles for the store. As soon as she spotted Juan, the legendary businesswoman gave him the friendliest smile (and in it Juan recognized Dr. Rozeman's artistry). Her enthusiasm was genuine: Juan was the first person to come into her department that day. Quickly hooking on the parachute, she led him across to the railing while instructing him in the basics of parachuting.

"In case the parachute should fail to open, you can be assured nothing will happen to you," said Nancy, always the optimist, as she tightened the last strap: "You'll only take a plunge in pleasantly warm water."

Indeed, at the center of the building's interior courtyard a cloud of steam was rising from the swimming pool down below that awaited our doorman, who, to please such an attentive, stylish, and also quite elderly lady, was already bracing himself for the jump. At that very moment, Nancy, with exquisite graciousness, handed him the parachute invoice for signing, and asked whether payment would be cash or credit.

"I didn't know I had to buy it," blurted Juan, pointing at the parachute.

"What!" bellowed Nancy, suddenly transformed into a wild beast. "Do you think this is a game you can play for free?"

"I thought it was only a demonstration," he apologized sheepishly.

"Idiot!" she shouted, getting even angrier. "Who would put on a parachute if not to use it?"

"You put it on me," justly protested our doorman.

And he began taking it off but, not being an expert in these matters, instead of releasing the strap, he pulled the rip cord, which opened the parachute. The lady was beside herself, screaming at Juan and threatening to sue him if he didn't pay for the merchandise right away. And so our doorman lifted himself gently over the railing and floated down to the celebrated swimming pool with the nice warm water. Disentangling himself as best he could from the parachute, he swam to the edge of the pool and ran out of the building. The burglar alarm, set off by Nancy Añeja herself, was already piercing the air.

Anyway, the doorman thought, finally safe in his room, it would have been impossible for him to buy anything right away: all his money was soaking wet.

· 18 ·

THE next day, New Year's Eve, Juan didn't have to go to work, not because it was a holiday (doormen still have to work on holidays) but because it was his day off. He felt obliged, however, to stop by the building in order to show the tenants that his functions surpassed what the regulations prescribed.

So at three o'clock, as always, Juan was at his post by the door in his impeccable uniform, but no one cared. The tenants were not at all surprised; many did not even realize it was his day off; some felt he might have come looking for extra tips, and even saw his presence at the door as an act of arrogance, showing his lack of appreciation for what they had already given him. Perhaps that was the reason why, despite Juan's extreme graciousness in greeting them that day, they barely returned his greeting, as if they intended to show him by their indifference something like "We've already given you enough, your flattery will not get you anywhere, you are not going to get another penny from us." And they kept going right on past him in all their holiday finery.

On his dinner break, Juan went up to visit Miss Mary Avilés, the woman he still thought of as his fiancée. From the money the tenants had given him, he had put a thousand dollars in an envelope; after his disastrous failure in trying to get her something from Nancy's, that was the present he wanted to give her. He also thought of encouraging her to use that money for a trip south, maybe to Florida, where the tropical climate could perhaps lift her spirits.

In spite of the intense cold, Mary's window was wide open. She was sitting half-naked on the windowsill in the hope that she would catch acute pneumonia and die. It had started snowing, and her hair was frosted white. The chilly blast of wind coming through the window had knocked down practically everything inside, including a floor lamp. With some relief Juan thought that even her pet rattlesnake must have retreated to a faraway corner.

Our doorman approached Mary Avilés, holding the envelope with the money in his outstretched hand. She stared blankly at him, took the envelope, and read aloud what her so-called lover had written:

Happy New Year.
Juan

This was all Juan had dared to write, and even this short phrase had cost him a lot of anguish. Wasn't it, in a sense, an insult to wish Mary Avilés a "happy" New Year? At least she didn't seem offended, though she didn't seem pleased either. Perched on the edge of an abyss, and with the wind piercing her bones, she looked at Juan, opened the envelope, saw what was inside, and returned it to him.

"I really appreciate it, but I can't accept it," she said.

"Why?" Juan asked her simply.

"Because I'm not going to need it and you will," she replied; and perhaps to please the doorman, she got down from the window, closed it, and went over to the sofa to lie down.

"You could take some time off for a trip south," said the doorman, with instant regret: down south was precisely where her parents lived, and she despised them.

And yet, Mary Avilés did not seem offended by his advice.

"I don't like to travel," was all she said, and lying back on the couch, she closed her eyes.

Though the window was now shut, it was still too wintry inside. Juan tried covering her with a quilt.

"No thanks," she said, lifting her hand, and again closed her eyes.

It seemed obvious that for now Mary Avilés wasn't the least bit interested in the doorman's company, and that only made him feel more depressed. Though the others had completely ignored him, he had expected something different, at least from Mary Avilés. How could it be, he wondered, that she failed to notice that they shared a similar fatalism (and loneliness) that created an unspoken bond between them? If the doorman had welcomed with enthusiasm the idea of being engaged to Mary Avilés, it wasn't because she attracted him physically more than any other woman — in fact, none had attracted him greatly — but because in a mysterious yet real way he felt, and somehow knew, that this particular young woman was his soul mate. With this in mind (as he recorded in his notes), Juan tried sitting beside her on the sofa. But Mary Avilés did not make room for him.

"Really it isn't you who should be giving me a present," she said. "On the contrary, I'm the one who should give you something. Forgive me for being so distracted and not having done it sooner. In the drawer over there," and she pointed, "is some money for you. Take it."

"I didn't come here looking for a tip," Juan blurted, visibly offended, and stood up.

That offer of money meant he was again being put back in his place as a lowly doorman, without the right to bother the tenants, much less on a holiday. But just as Juan was about to leave, Mary Avilés made another of her vague gestures, which Juan interpreted as plea for him to stay. And since she didn't mention the money again, he thought he could at least stay with her a few minutes longer.

Juan had never had much to say to the young woman, from the point of view of what we might call a normal relationship; nor did he have much to say to anybody, compared to the usual way that people can chat with each other for hours on end. His mission, as he wrote in his notebook, was not that at all. Instead, it was to listen, and by listening, to try to understand people. With this understanding he could possibly lead them to that distant door. . . . Yet with Mary Avilés the situation was more difficult, for how could he listen to her conversation when she barely spoke at all? In their stillborn dialogues, the silence itself seemed to demand words, even the most conventional ones, to validate it. No words were being said, though, and the doorman realized it was useless; he had to leave. But on a day like today, he was telling himself, people need to talk. In some more or less conscious way, people need to sum up their year, either with a word, a joke, or a scream. The inventory need not be exhaustive, but it is essential. It shows us what we lack and encourages the quest for fulfillment.

But for Mary Avilés, if anything was missing from her inventory, it was precisely the yearned-for nothingness that fate, with its eternal irony, seemed to deny her.

For more than half an hour sitting next to Mary Avilés on the couch, Juan kept silent as he waited for a word — even a single syllable — that would save him, that would save her. But the word did not come. The stark desolation that had always accompanied our doorman was, like so many times in the past, about to explode. The sky was growing dark.

We have already pointed out that our doorman was no great conversationalist, but instead a person who knew how to listen to others; and yet he did like (or couldn't resist the need) to improvise strange solitary speeches. He preferred to practice them in front of the tall mirror in the lobby or in the building's inner courtyard, where his words echoed loudly, and he, the doorman, would take them up again, thus carrying on a peculiar exchange of voices that sometimes lasted for his entire break. However, during the past few months in his job as doorman, these curious lapses into delirium, which elicited some of the tenants' complaints we have on file, became not only more frequent but also more incoherent. Precisely on that New Year's Eve of 1990, the speech delivered at Mary Avilés's apartment took on such mysterious overtones that, because of the singular importance of that day in the doorman's life (as we shall see), some of its fragments are worth reproducing here.

As the pale winter twilight filtered through the window of Mary Avilés's apartment, Juan moved directly to a mirror on the wall (we were watching him from the supposedly vacant apartment next door), and began declaiming:

Falling, falling, the ground awaits us, puppets writing in the snow, muffled shrieks, fixed stares, wires and cables, and you plunging toward them, you plunging toward them, what do you feel? Downward, plunging downward, palm trees rotting beneath the polluted state reservoirs, more silent screams. Your ear falls off, the other ear comes off, the third ear falls, your head suddenly gasping in the mud, suffocating, the ice penetrates your nose, deeper, deeper. What do you feel? Falling, falling, falling, and it was the light; now I'm telling you: of blood and snow, coming out of your eyes and through your teeth, of pigs squealing, palm fronds woven into ladles, frozen coconut fronds in the shape of cages, shadows of green fronds that are cages, plastic cages, well-lit cages, spotless cages ... And outside, mud that burns, fire that consumes, everything frozen. Juan, Juan, beloved Juan, they are calling you again, what, what have you done, what have you done? ... Fire that burns, fire that consumes, everything frozen, beloved Juan. Nothing. Still you have done nothing. Neither for nor against them, nothing to save them. Nothing to save you. All noise, the same stupidity, the same old woman with huge teeth, a single white shroud, a single shroud over roofs and cars, hats and noses. Like that, closing in on them, they said. Falling, falling, falling, I in the middle of a beacon of light, teeth coming toward me; a phosphorescent glow holds out its arms to me, coming closer and closer, closer and closer. Wherever you turn: the same old woman, a huge skeleton calling us and whether you want to or not, you paint its eyebrows! ... Loving Juan, beloved Juan, the horses are gone and the leaves and your disciples have not come down yet to the sea! You still don't exist. The snow is piling on the sidewalks and you have to scrape it off ... and they have been expecting you for two thousand years. Loving? Being loved? Loving? ... Don't make me laugh. Very expensive teeth. So you can smile at them and sprinkle salt on the street. If you could, you would have a neck that turned full-circle, but to see what? to see what?: to see that I am searching for those who search, knowing that they are not really searching, and in a palm grove I bury my own corpse. Armed divers, five thousand men, still underwater, they are afraid I might escape. Five thousand men, I don't want to keep repeating the same meek gestures, nor do I want all of you to keep forcing me to repeat them. "I am the door!" I shout from the middle of the ocean, from beneath the water. "I am the door!" Between the giant leaves I hide from the sun to be born again. So you are the door? Idiot.... Five thousand ashes. It's me: I haven't forgotten the password. Open up! I haven't forgotten the password. On the sun-baked Malecón — the Sea Wall, on the rampart, on the parapet, on the treetops, or out on the ice, forty days or longer on the sand: I haven't forgotten the password. Open up! Open up! To Capernaum.... You are the door. And only those who escape shall prevail; the rest will live in hatred and renunciation. It is my flesh, it is my flesh, they were telling me, and I was telling them, partake of it.... But, first, go out running, swimming, flying. Then we shall see, you will see, we will see, they will see: then we shall see horses and elephants, we shall see skies and corridors, bubbling springs, climbing vines and deserts, and the crab sign in the moon. He was telling me. And they were afraid....

Here the doorman interrupted his extraordinary speech, for the rattlesnake's rattle was whirring, and it sounded much too close, much too loud and powerful to be ignored, regardless of the young man's excited state of mind.

Instinctively, Juan got up on a chair and stood there for a few minutes; then, after making sure the creature was nowhere nearby, he stepped down and returned to Mary Avilés. He wanted at least to say goodbye to her with a kind word, and to beg her, as always, to be more careful of her life. And so he did. But Mary Avilés wasn't listening. Her eyes were wide open and there was a shade of triumph in her smile. Our doorman called her several times, then put his ear to her chest. He heard only the hair-raising whirring of the rattlesnake slithering away slowly out of the room. Apparently Mary Avilés had finally succeeded in leaving this world.

Letting out a scream, Juan ran into the hallway. He screamed so loudly that everyone in the building, despite the New Year's Eve racket, could not avoid hearing his wailing cry.

NONE of the tenants was surprised by the death of Mary Avilés. Quite the contrary. The super's wife, for months, had kept them well informed of the young woman's repeated suicide attempts, and they felt a certain relief when they learned that, finally, she had accomplished her objective. Even the police, after checking their files on her, limited themselves to a routine investigation. According to procedure, they posted a guard in the hallway, who forbade anyone to enter the apartment until the body had been removed; but since everyone knew about the rattlesnake, nobody dared go in except the doorman, who was ordered to leave after answering the policeman's questions. Juan really wanted to stay there next to Mary, but after several attempts the officer still did not let him stay. Juan finally realized that when a policeman asks you to leave, you had better disappear.

Still in a stupor, he went out into the street. He took a train (the ride was free on New Year's Eve) and got off in midtown Manhattan, where he was swept along by the throngs of revelers. At Rockefeller Center a gigantic pine tree, cut down on some mountainside, was now festooned with lights sparkling above wire angels blowing their mute trumpets; though, had the trumpets really been playing, the hubbub of cars and people would have drowned them out.

All along Fifth Avenue, the most luxurious window displays in the world revealed monumental electronic dolls portraying all kinds of Christmas scenes and legends. Against the leaden sky, typical of winter in New York, burst the first sprays of multicolored fireworks. . . . Juan wandered all the way down to Times Square and blended in with the sea of upturned heads staring expectantly at the One Times Square Building. A large, brightly lit clock would strike at midnight, with a huge red ball sliding down from the skyscraper's tallest spire. Below, at only twenty minutes to twelve, the roaring crowd was pressing together tighter and tighter. From the far corner of the crowded square somebody, clearly with criminal thoughtlessness, tossed up a bottle that certainly had to land on someone's head. This provoked the mounted police to plow violently into the masses, their horses almost trampling those people caught in the frenzied waves trying to get out of the way.

When one of the surges passed by our doorman, he felt an expert hand poking into one of his pockets. As the avalanche receded, Juan discovered that the pocket where he had put all his Christmas money was empty, and he experienced a sense of relief. But he quickly realized not all his money was gone; in his other pocket was still the envelope filled with what he had tried to give Mary Avilés. Since this sum was still intact, he pushed himself back into the crowd, which was now swarming in the opposite direction since another bottle had just shattered on someone's head. Juan was being pushed and shoved by the new stampede; but in the momentary calm that followed, our doorman was disappointed to find that this time no hands had emptied his pocket, so he pushed again into the multitude, which was growing in excitement as it watched the great clock. Without any fear, Juan moved toward a gang of youths who looked like professional pickpockets, and he even pulled some bills halfway out of the envelope to make them a really tempting target; but now even the billfold artists were focusing entirely on the hands of the giant clock as they approached midnight. After seeing that no one was going to steal his money, which he suddenly wanted to be rid of, Juan thought it was probably best to return to the building where he worked and leave the cash by the entrance. This idea quickly became a desire that then bore down on him like a command, almost as if the door itself were calling out to him. Now, of course, instead of trying to mingle with the crowd, he tried to get away. And here he was, right in the middle of Times Square. Juan started shoving and being shoved, pushing and being pushed, until he broke through the solid line of police trying to put some order in the reigning chaos. He managed somehow to get to a train and headed back toward his workplace.

He arrived at the building about ten minutes before midnight. In the middle of the deserted lobby he saw the shimmering Christmas tree with all its beautiful ornaments. The mechanical birds were chirping away, imitating — who knows why? he thought — the song of mockingbirds. Juan took out the envelope with the $1,000 and laid it beside the big glass door, where it could easily be spotted by the first tenant who came in. Still in a daze, he stood motionless while his face changed color with the intermittent flashes of the Christmas tree lights. Filtering through the lower floors he could hear strains of music mixed with the laughter of the tenants and their guests, and other noises — cheers, clapping, the popping of bottles being uncorked, small firecrackers, and the piercing shrieks of children who, because of the holiday, were being allowed to jump around the carpeted hallways. The doorman could also make out echoes of dog barks, chirps, meows, and grunts of other animals, but amid the din it was impossible to tell exactly where they were coming from. . . . Time was ticking by — it was now only three or four minutes to midnight — the music, the dancing, the laughter, all of the uproar was peaking and seemed to converge into a shout coming from the whole building rather than any particular spot. It almost seemed as if these people, and with them the whole city, were trying to squeeze into the final minutes of the year everything they had wanted to do but not done during the whole year, trying to fulfill (and exhaust) in three minutes all their unrealized desires of three hundred and sixty-four days; trying to capture in those three, now two, now one minute, all of time; all the time that, unawares, they had let slip by. . . . *Before it's too late, before it's too late, before it's too late* this unanimous bellow seemed to be saying. . . . And even though Juan knew like everyone else that in just a few seconds it would be midnight, it was impossible for him to hold back a shudder of terror when the twelve bells began to chime, full and powerful and marking time implacably lost forever. And immediately the whole city announced with its myriad visual and auditory devices that it was now twelve midnight of the year 1990. The sky overflowed with explosions of light. And when the outcry reached a climax amplified by ten million voices, the now familiar sensation of despair and suffocation, of unbearable frustration, once again took hold of our doorman. Another year gone by, and he had not yet found the door; worse yet, he had not even been able to convince anyone of the importance of finding it. . . . And so the cries of revelry from the tenants in his building and from the inhabitants of the whole city were for Juan not a reflection of their joy, but a desperate scream of reproach aimed, of course, directly at him, the doorman. And looking at himself once more in the tall mirror in the lobby, in his splendid uniform with golden buttons and braid, his high cap and white gloves, Juan experienced the horrible but clear vision of himself as a clown — rather than a savior — just another lackey in the ridiculous scheme of things. The lowest of the lackeys! Forced to repeat the same pompous gestures and so-called courtesies for all those people who, because they could afford the luxury of a doorman, felt entitled to walk with their noses held high in the air.

Then, he thought, now beginning to mumble to himself, if that's the way things are (how they seemed to him at the time), if there's nothing more, nothing beyond the eternal opening and closing of doors for people to come and go from nowhere to nowhere, what sense did it make to keep on doing this? What sense did it make to go on living? . . . Very soon (and now he was speaking out loud) I will go up to wish them a Happy New Year, to drink with them, get the pat on the back, and maybe even the quick, patronizing handshake. NO! he shouted, so loudly that if the tenants and their guests didn't hear him, it was only because their own racket drowned out everything else. And right there, next to the big glass door, the doorman stripped off his uniform, threw down the gloves and hat, and dressed himself again in the street clothes he kept in the doorman's closet. He decided at that very moment (whether it was one of total lucidity or utter insanity) to abandon not just that building, not just that city, but rather, like Mary Avilés, the whole universe. *I will vanish and in that way at least I'll no longer be a part of this mechanized world that is going nowhere....* He had left behind his homeland, a world *"to which I not only will not return but which I will not even want to remember."* However, this other reality he had adopted was also, for him, a world he would have to alter in order to make it bearable. And if it was true that he couldn't stand the world he had left behind (which, in spite of himself, he had not been able to forget), then it was also true that he could not fit into the reality he had found. And if none of it could be transformed to match his aspirations — he was thinking out loud on his way out — is there a place for me? . . . What sense does it make for me to stay here, or there, or anywhere? . . .

"Good evening," said a feminine voice coming from the elevator. "Good evening," it repeated in a definitely British accent, a bit louder this time, which left Juan with no choice but to turn around and answer the greeting.

But nobody came out of the open elevator. There was only Cleopatra, the Warrems' famous Egyptian dog. The animal stepped forward serenely, approached the doorman, repeated in impeccable English, "Good evening." And since Juan was still stunned, the dog spoke again:

"I really hope it does not surprise you to learn that I talk, for I would be truly offended."

"No, no, of course not. Not at all," said the doorman, even more amazed.

"Good," continued Cleopatra, "because there is not much time now. I took the opportunity to escape from the apartment during all the New Year's nonsense, but they will start looking for me any minute now" — and the distinguished lady-dog pointed upstairs just with her eyes — "so our conversation must be very brief. I heard what you were saying and I heard your cries. They — " and again she glanced toward the ceiling, "fortunately, heard nothing. . . . Listen to me: I and a group of friends need very much to speak with you. It is very important. We have agreed to meet with you tomorrow morning at ten in the basement. So pick up your uniform and the money, and go and get some rest. Remember, tomorrow morning in the basement. Goodbye."

Quickly, but without losing her composure for a moment, Cleopatra turned toward the elevator and disappeared. Watching her walk away, the doorman could not tell whether he was astonished or excited. He picked up his uniform and the money and headed for his room on the other side of the city.

W E interrupt this narrative to warn our readers that if you even faintly expect some kind of rational or scientific explanation (or whatever you might call it) concerning Cleopatra's attitude or powers, we hasten to ask that you completely dismiss any such hopes. The reason we can't explain these happenings is very simple: we don't have any explanation. And, as we said earlier, we have limited ourselves to transcribing events as they were taking place and as they were recorded. Remember, too, as we have also said before, that we are a million individuals. Thus our account is really a synthesis of all that we have seen, read, heard, or perceived, including even the psychological states of our main character, the doorman; states of mind that our psychologists (incidentally, the best in the country) have been able to decipher from our information. But it is not our wish to embellish with fantastic or pseudo-scientific commentary what we simply do not understand.

Our main objective, among other very important ones that we will soon bring to light, is to summarize our doorman's case in writing, in the hope that some future interpreters more enlightened than ourselves may someday be able to understand it.

It seems almost unnecessary to remind any such future interpreter that, as a matter of principle (and it has not been without difficulty), we would have preferred to present our case history originally in Spanish, even though practically all of the dialogues, monologues, tapes, notes, interviews, and other original documents are, of course, in English.

At the present time, even our grief is being expressed in a tongue still foreign to us.

· The Door ·

BUT what would the door be like? Naturally, the door itself was not what counted — it was the determination to go beyond it and discover what lay waiting on the other side. However, its shape, and the kind of door it was, would have a tremendous influence on those who approached it.... A door like a tower, carved and painted by the angels themselves? A graceful and stately gate, like that of a palace? A majestic one, like the entrance to a cathedral? Or one so evanescent, almost invisible, as to be detectable only by the chosen ones? ... A door toward which Roy Friedman, jubilant, might rush, leaving at the threshold his heavy load of toffees and gooey sweets, followed close behind by Joseph Rozeman, who for the first time would smile toothlessly. A door. A door Brenda Hill might go through completely sober, and a door beside which Scarlett Reynolds, before passing through, might leave behind her fortune and her rag dog. A door where Juan could already envision the two Oscar Timeses entering completely relaxed, and even the noisy Pietri family and Stephen Warrem, all engaged in friendly conversation with Arthur Makadam. A door where Mr. Skirius would suddenly rematerialize and — fascinated by that marvelous invention, the door — would decide to go through. An arch beneath which even Cassandra Levinson might pass, recognizing the error of her dehumanized philosophy, and make a fresh start. A door that, without having to touch it, John Lockpez might go through, and also realize the absurdity of his militant fanaticism. A very special door for

Mary Avilés, who, with a conspiring wink, would summon the doorman so they might cross the threshold together. . . . But what would the door look like? How might it be ornamented? With marble? Reliefs? Paintings? Ivory? Statues? . . . A door, a door. A carved door? A floating one? Square or round? Simple or grand? . . . A door, a door. A plain wooden frame? Or an imposing, convex structure? A spot of light among the clouds? Or a small opening on the wall? . . . Yes, a door, a very special kind of door. But, once crossed, what then?

·PART TWO·

· 20 ·

WE have now reached the most difficult point in this work, based (as we have already said) on the reports of our informants and the notes our doorman wrote. We don't really know what style to adopt in order to make our story more believable without, at the same time, interfering with its apparently fantastic qualities.

Of course, as soon as we expressed our concern about the problems of literary composition, quite understandable for a community not exactly devoted to literature, we were criticized (even in writing) for having undertaken the recounting of these events because we are an anonymous team of nonspecialists. And even though we were elected by the majority, there are a few individuals in our community who are, or at least claim to be, real writers, and who think they could perform these duties better than we can.

Why, then, as the usual dissatisfied minority (common in every free society) keeps reproaching us, why don't we, for example, seek the assistance of someone like Guillermo Cabrera Infante, or Heberto Padilla, or Severo Sarduy, or Reinaldo Arenas, people who are better suited for this undertaking? Why (continues the reproach by our nitpicking faultfinders) do we insist on reaching beyond our grasp or meddling in things that do not concern us, when we could avail ourselves of the help of true experts from our own community?

Our reason is very simple. With Guillermo Cabrera Infante this account would completely lose its essential meaning and would become a kind of tongue-twister, a clownish stunt, or linguistic wordplay, loaded with more or less ingenious frivolities. Heberto Padilla would seize upon every line to interject his hypertrophic ego, so that instead of giving us the trials and tribulations of our doorman, the text would be transformed into an apologia for Padilla, always putting himself at the center of attention, without allowing even the most insignificant insect its moment of glory. And in our case, even the insects have a part to play, as we shall see later. . . . And as for Reinaldo Arenas, his declared and blatant homosexuality would contaminate every aspect — texts and events, descriptions and characters — completely clouding over the objective nature of this episode, which neither is nor pretends to be a case of sexual pathology. On the other hand, if we had settled on Sarduy, the whole affair would have become a glittering neobaroque bauble and nobody would understand a word. Therefore, in spite of our clumsiness with this kind of work, we feel we must go ahead with our project on our own, come what may.

· 21 ·

DURING the rest of that evening, the thirty-first of December of 1990, our doorman lay in his room, unable to fall asleep. It still seemed incredible to him that he had actually heard a dog talk. So, even though he did not sleep at all, when he got up he thought he had had a nightmare. To find out whether that was true, he returned to the building where he worked and, at ten o'clock sharp, went down to the basement, hoping to find it deserted.

But it wasn't. In spite of his strict punctuality, all the animals from the building and surrounding areas were already there waiting for him. There was a momentary hush as Juan entered, until Cleopatra broke the silence by addressing the guest:

"I do not think it necessary to introduce my friends to you: you know many of them and the rest you will get to know very soon. Besides, we have little time, and not a moment to lose. The reason we have invited you to this meeting is this: We have all noticed how concerned you are for the people who live in this building, but we have never seen you take the same interest in us."

"Neither the same nor any at all!" broke in Brenda Hill's cat, arched and bristling.

"You can't say that," interceded one of the mongrel females belonging to Mr. Lockpez. "He has run his hand over my spine several times."

"Spine! Do you think so little of yourself as to say you have a spine, while they have backs?" Brenda Hill's cat retorted sharply.

Since others were already starting to enter the discussion, Cleopatra, with a fierce bark, demanded silence and, addressing the doorman, continued: "I hope it does not surprise you too much to learn that my friends speak, as I do, your own language. We do this, of course, so that you can understand us, but at other times, both as a matter of principle and for our personal safety, we speak in our own language, which I hope you will learn very soon. . . . But, for now, let us return to the subject of this risky meeting. One of the things we wanted to tell you is that none of the people you are so concerned about has understood a word you have said; worse yet, they have not listened, and they are even planning to throw you out of the building."

"No, they aren't planning," corrected one of the Pietris' five chihuahuas while she removed the earphones from her ears. "They already have it all planned. I myself heard the super say so."

"Well," responded Cleopatra, "that means we have less time than we thought."

"No time! We have no time!" the five chihuahuas cried in unison. Then they put their headphones back in place, swaying and barking rhythmically in five-part harmony, at which point Cleopatra growled fiercely and again demanded silence.

"We have a proposal for you," proceeded the canine Egyptian princess, facing the doorman. "First, we want you to listen to us; then, to think it over; and afterward, to join us."

At her words, the basement filled with growls, meows, chirps, and barks of approval.

"Once we have reached agreement," continued Cleopatra above the uproar, "we intend to look for a solution, or in your words, for *a way out* or *a door*. A door for you and for us. Not for them, the tenants: they do not need one. They have not even realized they are prisoners."

"But I have!" broke in the shrill voice of one of the parrots, fluttering about tied to her partner. "And how! I have been locked up for five long years!"

"And with stale bread crumbs and sour milk for food," added the other parrot.

"Don't try to tell us you're worse off than we are," yapped the five chihuahuas in chorus, again taking off their earphones. "At least you," one of the chihuahuas declared, "the only thing you have to do is go around perched on your hoop and nibble at bread crumbs. But we, besides being shut in, have to dance around and go about sniffing and nudging our masters with our snouts."

"Not snouts, noses!" protested Brenda Hill's fierce female cat. "Or do you really consider yourselves inferior to them?"

"Yes, they think they are inferior," piped in one of the super's rats. "Otherwise they wouldn't spend their lives kissing their masters' feet and doing all kinds of monkey business."

"Monkey business?" very quickly put in Mr. Makadam's orangutan, who now lived in hiding in a deserted tunnel beneath the garden. "They have no business acting like monkeys. And speaking about 'monkey business,' I notice this expression is always used with a sneer. It is taken for granted that all we do is imitate the movements, gestures, and silly things people do. A simple test would be enough to clear up this confusion, which is offensive to us. Who came first? Human beings or apes? Even humans accept that it is logical to think that we came first, millions of years before them. And so, dear friends, who is imitating whom?"

"Certainly," hissed Mary Avilés's snake, "and for the same reason, since we snakes came into the world before apes and before humans as well, everybody imitates *us*. Oh, and speaking of men, since one of them happens to be here now," and half raising her body, the snake gazed directly into Juan's eyes, "I would like to make clear to him that it wasn't I who killed Miss Avilés, as people have been saying. Never once did I bite her. She committed suicide, she took twenty-seven potassium cyanide tablets. In fact, by the time you got to her apartment yesterday, Mary Avilés had already poisoned herself. I don't know how you failed to notice that her face was turning green. I even tried to warn you with a loud rattle but, naturally, you thought I was preparing to attack you. . . ."

"And why didn't you speak to me, as you are doing now?" complained the doorman, dejected. "Perhaps we could have saved her."

"I did" — the snake reared up high — "but you ignored me completely. All you cared about was making your big speech. If you hadn't been — "

"Enough!" growled Cleopatra, pinning the serpent with her fiery violet eyes. "First, you had orders not to speak to the doorman in his language before this meeting; and second, we did not come here to waste time on silly arguments about things we can no longer change. Our purpose is to rise above our differences and come to an agreement. Now, putting aside the question of whether animals or humans are superior, the fact is that we are not humans and up to now they are the ones who, for the most part, have ruled the world. So we need to be united and we also need an ally in the enemy camp, someone who could, in a word, 'represent' us and whom we can help in turn. And we have agreed, after observing you for a while, that you are that person," concluded Cleopatra, looking at the doorman.

"Yes, you, you! What do you say?" several animals shouted at the same time, surrounding the doorman. "We have so much to tell you!"

Cleopatra turned toward the door, sniffed, and then addressed the meeting in a tone of urgency.

"I understand how anxious you are to tell the doorman all your grievances. But we shall never reach an accord this way, and our time is up for today. Our next meeting is scheduled for Friday at the same time. The first speaker will be the dove, and no interruptions permitted. Now, return to where you came from as if nothing had happened."

The dogs, cats, parrots, the orangutan and the rest of the animals, including Cassandra Levinson's bear, the doves, the rats, and even the turtles (carried by the ape) all disappeared from the basement as fast as they could. But on their way out they formed a large circle around our doorman and, in a chorus of yelps, meows, screeches, chirps, and growls, gave him an excited farewell. Then the rest of Mr. Lockpez's animals retied themselves to their partners and disappeared from view.

They left in the nick of time, for the super, who had heard the strange noises, was coming down to investigate. But thanks to his customary sluggishness, all he found was our doorman.

"What are *you* doing here at this hour?" snapped the super, obviously annoyed.

"I came to wash windows for Mrs. Brenda Hill," replied our doorman.

"Since when did Mrs. Hill's windows move to the basement?"

"I was looking for a rag or a sponge."

"There is none of that around here. If there were, you'd have to see me first before taking it. Is that clear?"

"Perfectly," murmured Juan.

But the super thought he detected a tone of defiance in his voice, and perhaps even a trace of eagerness.

"Well, anyway, I'll have to report this to the management," he said with a worried expression, and he slammed the door behind him.

· 22 ·

IN spite of the super's reaction and his threat of reporting the incident to the management (a threat he was sure to make good), our doorman felt as if he had been under a spell. The animals had talked to him; what's more, it seemed that they had unanimously chosen him — and him alone — to hear their troubles and to give them help. As a result, Juan told himself, not only would he have to listen and find a solution to the tenants' problems (trying to lead each one of them along a different path toward the right exit — or perhaps entrance?), but he would also have to help their pets and the other animals that had attended the meeting who had no masters, such as the rats, the squirrels, and even the fly that survived in the cold basement by hovering in the warm stream of the bear's breath.

After a quick lunch at a nearby cafeteria and though it was not time yet for his shift to begin, Juan went back to his post by the door. In a mixed mood, half happy and half worried, he was soon lost in his own thoughts.

In all truth, we must admit, some of the complaints filed against Juan were justified. During the last few weeks, his brooding and his absent-mindedness had been apparent to everyone. On several occasions the tenants had had to open the door themselves because, although the doorman was physically there, he seemed to be in another world. It still seems hard to understand why the super didn't show the doorman any of the letters of complaint; perhaps it suited his own interests not to alert him, so that the young man would continue neglecting his duties.

But if Juan's absent-mindedness, sometimes bordering on total distraction, had already become notorious, it reached an alarming level after his first meeting with the animals. He had been so powerfully impressed by that gathering, and so touched by their overwhelming reception (how could he ever forget their intense eyes, so full of trust?) that when the tenants started to come down for their walks around seven o'clock, Juan, lost in a state of confusion or wonderment, rather than greeting Brenda Hill as usual, greeted her cat instead. And when Mr. Lockpez came by with a dove, the symbol of his purity, well secured on his shoulder, Juan did not return the minister's ever-eager handshake, but grasped the feet of the dove.

The tenants' amazement grew even more when they saw the animals' euphoric responses to our doorman's friendly gestures. Dr. Rozeman's three lady-dogs smiled at him more eloquently than usual; the Oscar Timeses' rabbit, in spite of its timid nature, dared to sniff the doorman's foot (miraculously, without suffering an attack from the bulldog, who would surely have seized the chance to catch it off guard). Even Mr. Pietri's vulgar chihuahuas, always led out by Pascal Junior, stopped their yelping and sassy swaying when they passed by our doorman. Finally, when the representatives of the Church of Love of Christ Through Friendly and Constant Contact returned from their walk, one of the parrots said to Juan, "See you later" in much better English than that of its master, Mr. Lockpez. At this point the doorman could not hold back any longer, and in his Spanish-flavored English, wished the parrot good night. Fortunately, since it's natural for these animals to imitate human voices, what surprised Mr. Lockpez was not that the parrot had spoken, but that it did not repeat, as it always did, the religious gibberish it had so thoroughly learned from its master.

The only animal to pass by Juan with complete indifference was Cleopatra, who marched ahead escorted by a solemn Mr. Warrem. Not until she was inside the elevator did she dare give the doorman a quick, conspiratorial glance as if to say, "Don't forget." Of course not, Juan said to himself, and bowed toward the elevator as it was going up.

· 23 ·

THE dove began in this manner:
"I appreciate being honored as the first speaker in this meeting, and since my own circumstances are very similar to those of many of you here today, I think I may be able to speak for all of us. It is also important to see that the doorman has joined us, because I have known him for a long time and feel pity for his situation (the same pity he also feels for me). Without him, perhaps we might never be able to choose the appropriate course of action or, having made our choice, not be capable of carrying it out. In another sense, the doorman and I are (except for feathers and other insignificant details) almost the same person, or animal, whichever he prefers. We are both creatures of the tropics now living in a climate that is unnatural, almost hostile to us. We both miss our warm, sunny lands, and what is most important, we are both prisoners. He is the prisoner of conditions that for many reasons he cannot escape and of a past that, no matter how hard he tries, he cannot leave behind. It is not that he wants to go back to that past: he wants to leave this place (just as much as I, just as much as all of us do). Therefore, the purpose of this meeting can only be to decide whether to remain prisoners or to escape. Of course if we are prisoners (and who can deny it?), flight, or at least the attempt to flee, seems to be our only choice. However, flight is what I would like to put in question. I myself, from the moment I was taken prisoner, have thought of nothing else. . . . As a result of all the time I have been in captivity, I have gradually lost agility in all

my muscles, lightness in flight, keenness of vision, even the knack for eluding traps and shotgun fire, and perhaps the persistence necessary to find food for my own sustenance. And all of you have also lost these or similar skills, much as you would like to deny it. . . ." The dove fastened her gaze for a moment on almost every animal in the assembly, as well as on the doorman. "Besides, why deny it, I fear the cold weather I will have to suffer during the flight until I reach, if I ever do, warmer regions. Of course, I suppose if we decide to flee we'll be looking for a warm region, not one of the Poles, which would be pretty much where we are living right now. It also terrifies me to think of the possibility of being hunted and roasted. Of course, not everybody here has flesh as highly prized as mine. . . . And then, after all, I ask myself: Can we really live in a place we left so long ago? Here, at least, we have a certain amount of comfort and even some security. We don't have to go hungry, and we can say that, on the whole, no one is trying to kill us. But out there, would the other animals we still call *savage*, to our shame, accept us? And even if they did, wouldn't there be on their part a silent reproach, and on ours, a constant feeling of insecurity? Could we at this stage still adapt to the risks of a free, but also dangerous, life? . . . Yes, I am well aware that to begin this meeting by questioning these points may seem irresponsible and defeatist on my part, and some might even think it has been my intention to dampen everybody's enthusiasm. But allow me to say that I, like all of you, have often thought of escape. I even made an attempt one morning. I had no idea which direction to take, it was getting colder and colder, and, in a few hours, I was exhausted. Even to find my way back seemed too difficult. I discovered it would have been embarrassing to find myself in a group with other doves: my feathers no longer glisten as they used to, and I can't coo anymore — my song has turned into a dull, guttural sound that people find charming because they don't know any better. . . . All in all, then, I'm not saying definitely no, but I'm not saying yes either. My only question is, can we succeed? And if we succeed, can we survive?" At this point the dove paused briefly to peck at a flea under her wing, before concluding in a steadier voice: "There is no doubt that a man as intelligent as the doorman, in case we decide to escape, will support the idea of heading for a lush tropical land, warm but breezy, where we can settle in the treetops. Nevertheless, let me emphasize in conclusion that any decision we make should be carefully thought out."

As soon as the dove finished her speech, the squirrel, the ape, and the parrots loudly voiced their approval of relocating to the treetops in some tropical land. Yet, immediately one of the turtles stepped forward to say he too approved of moving to a warmer climate but, instead of treetops, they ought to find a lagoon.

"A lagoon surrounded by trees, to provide us of course with food and a fresh breeze, but not for us to go climbing around in, which is not very dignified and not very safe either. I know what I'm talking about," continued the turtle, "I'm the oldest one here. Let me explain. . . ."

Though the turtle's speech promised to be long, it was quickly cut short by the snake, who in a precise, sibilant tone declared that the perfect spot was naturally a hot climate, but on solid ground, or better still, on rocks.

"Subways and caves make the best homes," corrected the rat.

"The ocean is unquestionably the best place to live because it is the most spacious and consequently offers the greatest number of possibilities," asserted the two golden fish belonging to Mr. Lockpez, splashing about in the fishbowl the orangutan had brought down, but which the doorman was now holding because the ape couldn't keep still for a second, in spite of Cleopatra's icy stares.

"Up to now, the only thing I hear is *tropics*," protested the bear, "but I need snow, and I'm an important member of this group. Without my protection I don't think you can get very far."

"Trees! Giant bamboos and baobabs! That's what we want!" shrieked the orangutan.

"The ocean, the ocean! . . ." countered the golden fish, still splashing about in their small bowl.

"Caves!" proposed the rat.

"A lagoon!" commanded in unison the two turtles from Pastor Lockpez's menagerie.

Meanwhile, the super's five chihuahuas, no longer interested, wanted to break off the meeting and go home. It was time to eat and Mrs. Pietri would be looking for them.

But then Cleopatra, at once irate and serene, spoke up, saying that it was shameful to want to leave when the meeting had just started; that the issues to be discussed were of tremendous importance to everybody; and that the reason for the meeting was precisely to hear different opinions and to reach an agreement.

Calm was then restored and the rattlesnake was given the floor. She seemed greatly disturbed by the dove's speech.

· 24 ·

"I WILL be brief," said the snake, "since I don't need to tell you how much I suffered as a zoo animal (you cannot get any lower than that), and then as a morbid obsession for a psychopath like Miss Avilés. . . . My dear friends, the only thing we can have between humans and us is the greatest possible distance. If I haven't objected to the doorman almost presiding over this meeting it is only because my keen sensitivity — or my adrenaline, if you prefer — tells me that he is different from all the other humans we know. And because he is so different from the others we call *humanity* — and indeed I learned by heart many of the monologues he recited in the home of the late Mary Avilés — I am sure he will completely agree with me. Like the doorman, I too have devoted myself to observing people through a piece of glass: first, from my cage at the zoo; later, from the special cage Mary Avilés put me in when she wanted to take me out for a walk. So, whether being watched or not, I was studying them, and came to know them much better than they know me; they who say such stupid things about me. . . . My friends, the only way to keep humans happy is having the rest of creation, including other people, locked up behind bars. For them, everything we do is but a crude imitation of their actions; and it gives them pleasure to believe they are in control of the universe. They may be cruel and try to destroy us; or, being either practical or foolishly sentimental, they may try to save us. Whatever they do, they only act out of self-interest. So it is not a question of me being in a cage, but that we all are. And who is to blame, if not those fickle, war-like, and vile creatures, so conceited in their self-appointed role as masters of the world, a world they have converted into a gigantic zoo for their private enjoyment? We should force humans to retreat to small reservations or perhaps resign themselves to extinction, which, by the way, would be the best thing that could happen. Have you stopped to think how happy and peaceful our lives would be if mankind disappeared? . . . How could this extinction, or at least this retreat, be brought off? Through hatred and war. There is no other solution. Our race, the serpents of the world, are preparing for that war. Humans are well aware of our cleverness and our intentions, and that is why people have worked so hard to give us a bad name since the beginning of their history. You can't find a fable concerning us where we are not cast in a sinister role, naturally starting with the Bible, which is the greatest hoax invented by humans. The truth about us is completely the opposite of the way we are depicted in all those foolish stories. We are a noble race, so much so that before we attack we give fair warning with our characteristic rattle. Even when we have no intention of attacking, we politely signal our presence, to avoid alarming anyone. And what has such honesty earned us? Centuries, actually millennia, of nothing but persecution. Therefore, my proposal to our assembly is to require humans to retire to far-off regions under our strict supervision. I and the rest of my noble race offer our services for this deportation assignment. Picture for yourselves millions of rattlesnakes whirring their rattles in every city, using this sound to command humans to go wherever we choose. That is my opinion, and the opinion also, I am sure, of the doorman."

Thus ended the rattlesnake's speech. Juan then wanted a chance to reply and, raising his hand, looked at Cleopatra, as she obviously ruled over the meeting. But at that moment the rat, claiming her turn to speak, scurried to the middle of the floor.

25

T HE rat began as follows:

"My proposal, or whatever you want to call it, need not be long. I'm a practical type and don't like to waste time. You can see I don't wear any flashy ornaments, such as that stupid tail on the squirrel; much less, colored feathers like the parrot; and still less, foolish rattles like the snake, not to mention her pretentious load of *adrenaline*" — and the rat emphasized this word with a sardonic smile, raising her voice to drown out the immediate protests of the offended animals: "I've got what it takes! Teeth for gnawing! And with these teeth I'm ready to second the snake's motion, provided she is willing to shed her rattle, which could give us away! . . . We are fed up with all the traps and poisoned cheese that for so long have made life practically impossible for us. From now on, we're going to set the terms, which are these: People will live in the cities we select for them and will work there to produce all the garbage and other foods we need. We'll gnaw and nibble on these, and then we'll toss them the scraps so they can survive. We'll divide up the whole world among us; it's not for nothing that we are cosmopolitan types, like the doorman, who can survive just as well in cold or hot climates. He is surely one of our most important allies, and it was very smart to invite him to this meeting. The three of us, the snake, the doorman, and I, are obviously the best suited for this essential task. I must take exception, however, with the snake's idea of keeping humans at a distance. No, instead we should control them, live at their expense, and gnaw to our hearts' content. . . . A hatred as strong as our appetite will help keep our teeth always sharp and ready."

As a public demonstration of her prowess, the rat ended her speech by vigorously gnashing her teeth several times while she performed a frenzied dance of leaps and bounds in the middle of the assembly.

Our doorman once again raised his hand, surely to object to the rat's proposal, but Cleopatra had already given the nod to the turtle.

26

VERY slowly the turtle made his way to the center of the room, tied as usual to his companion, and his watery, blinking eyes seemed fixed on some distant point. He was going to speak for himself, his companion, and for the large family of turtles. This is what he had to say:

"To live for hatred is to live serving our enemy. To have an enemy is already to be only half ourselves, the other half always occupied by our enemy. Anyone who harbors a passion for destruction or the fear of being destroyed does not really live, but merely suffers a long-term agony. Compare the nervous and frightened expression in Mrs. Rat's face with the quiet dignity of my features, and judge for yourselves. Also compare the dangers threatening this creature's short, hazardous life with the peace and longevity of ours. I think the point is clear. Almost all of you, including the doorman, will doubtlessly side with my philosophy, which is simply the search for silence, serenity, and forgetting. Notice I am not speaking of *forgiving*, but actually *forgetting*. Forgiveness implies remembrance and, in a sense, to come to terms with someone you have hated or someone you have loved who has hurt you. Let us avoid these traps that people set for us, and search for a place where, removed from all these calamities, we can be ourselves. Let us go to a place where we can live our own lives, instead of being dependent, for whatever reasons, on human beings. The only means of escaping their reasoning is to ignore it. There must still be places where it is possible to be oblivious to human motives. My hundred-year-old instincts show me the path we must follow." Now the turtle stretched his neck, apparently pointing toward a corner in the basement. "We must go to a place where there is both land and water, for obvious reasons: all beings are amphibians, though this ability in some species has become seriously stunted. We are amphibians not only physically, but also in spirit. No one can survive in a single element, and those who can live in all of them are, no doubt, the most fortunate. Let us just for once take human beings, atrophied creatures as they are, as examples. Though people live on land, don't they always head for the water? For reasons they cannot understand (but we can), don't they manage to march in strange processions to the seashore? Note how they stop at the edge of the water and stay there for a while as if mesmerized.... What are they looking at? What are they after? What drives them to come from even the farthest corners of the earth to this encounter with the sea? They do not know it, but they are searching for themselves. They are looking for the other half of themselves that they lost either through suffering or from their own cowardice, and which belonged to the water. In this water, as in all waters, they hope to find their own reflection, an image that became distorted thousands of years ago. We can see them everywhere near the shore, as if in meditation. What are they longing for? For the union with the part of themselves they have lost. Quite often, some of them cannot resist and go underwater, but their weak and mutilated organs are no longer capable of responding as they would like to, and they perish. The more cowardly ones, those who dare not take the plunge, call the others *suicides*.... Let us not fear them or hate them. Let us forget them. In all truth, we should feel sorry for them. To feel compassion is not a bad idea, but only from a distance. After all, once we have returned to the vast aquatic expanses, they will not be able to annihilate us even if they try, and they will try. Could they ever, if they wanted, dry up the oceans? Could they possibly do without both the sea and the land? Don't you see that we are much better suited than human beings for living on this planet? In the specific case of my family, my glorious turtle ancestry, our survival for so many thousands of years provides ample proof. Consequently, our position in favor of retreat — silence, serenity, and forgetting — cannot be ignored."

BRAVO! Bravo!" cried one of the fish, whose turn it now was to speak. Then he plunged back into the water to catch his breath. "You are right," he said, surfacing. "Water is the most essential element. Nature had its reasons for making sure this world we live in would be defined by its water" — the golden fish ducked for a moment — "and not by its land, which occupies an insignificant space in comparison with all the oceans, seas, lakes, and rivers" — and after another ducking — "therefore, as a second motion, I propose that the name of this planet should be changed to represent its main element: Water!" After a gulp of air, he came up again: "Enough of Planet Earth! It's Planet Water from now on! That's what my family has called it since the beginning of time and, by the way, remember we are the largest community in the world." The speaker ducked and emerged again, "My status as fish thus gives me the broadest possible knowledge. . . ."

"I think that instead of *fish* you ought to call yourself *fished*, since even though you didn't take the bait, *fished you are!*" interrupted Brenda Hill's cat before Cleopatra could silence her.

"If anyone calls me *fished* because I am a temporary prisoner," argued the fish between bubbles, "then you, who has known only captivity, should not call yourself *cat* but *caught!*" — and with a sneer he dived in for air again. "Yes, speaking as a fish, and therefore as a representative of those who dominate the largest inhabited region of the globe, I am forced to conclude that it is the water (and not earth and water combined, as the turtle suggests) where we all ought to live. After all, if it's already difficult swimming both in the the ocean and in the rivers, it would be much harder to live in two completely opposite elements. Besides, by being always caught between times underwater and times on land, we would never be able to establish any permanent family or social ties. While in the water, we would long for solid ground, but once on land, we would want to be back in the water. Thus we would always be wavering and restless, and at the same time easy prey to countless enemies. Since we already know the earth is mostly water, why should we want to stay in tighter, more suffocating spaces?" By now the fish was actually gasping. He submerged once more to breathe, and continued: "In this regard I'm sure the doorman agrees with me. Whenever I'm taken out for a walk, and whenever the doorman visits Mr. Lockpez in his apartment, I watch him from my aquarium. The doorman is always looking out through the big glass door or through the windows, always searching for the spaciousness of the open sea. Even the sky, which he contemplates and observes so often, isn't it perhaps because of its color and vastness a reflection or a mirror of the sea itself?" After a long submersion, the fish returned with the following thesis: "Our doorman is a poor fish just like me, suffocating in this place. Just look at him, when you have a chance, behind all that glass in the lobby, enclosed in his fishbowl, desperately searching for a way to return to open waters." Then the fish swam all around the small aquarium. "Actually the doorman and I are almost the same person, or rather the same fish. Each of us is desperately going round and round in our own fishbowl, but always searching, always waiting. The doorman knows every inch of the big glass door in the lobby as well as I know every millimeter of this bowl. And yet we never stop looking out through our glass cages, hoping that one day something — the true waters, the deluge, the Flood itself! — might come to set us free. . . ." He now dived down and stayed down. The other golden fish bubbled up and continued: "I'm not going to deny that both the doorman and I have suffered here from severe depression almost every day. How many times, during my desperate imprisonment, have I wished I could jump out of my bowl into the sink, or even the toilet bowl, and rush through the pipes to reach the open sea. . . . Sheer madness, perhaps, but the doorman knows how difficult it is to control oneself. I also know how sometimes he has had to hold himself back in order not to run off and disappear into underground tunnels or any other city alleys leading nowhere. When I see him pacing back and forth inside his own glass cage, like me, searching for the oxygen that these enclosures do not provide us but rather steal from us, I feel a certain consolation: *I'm not alone, not alone,* I tell myself; *he is with me because he suffers just as I do. Someday we'll talk, and together we'll find a way out. . . .*"

"And so you see," continued the first fish while his companion descended to the bottom to recover, "you see us finally together, him holding me with hands that will soon become fins, and all of us here in search of a solution, of a salvation that can only be found in the water. . . ."

The speech by the fish ended with a resounding outcry of protest. Only the other fish agreed with the idea of going to live at the bottom of the sea. Even the pigeon, who did not have a vote in the assembly because she was represented by the dove (just as the lizards were represented by the snake), began fluttering around above the gathering, and said that if the place they chose was to be determined by its physical size, then it would be logical to side with the birds' proposal. "Can there be," asked the flying pigeon, "any place more spacious than the sky, that is, infinity itself?"

But at a royal command from Cleopatra, the pigeon returned to her spot on top of the bear's head, and the meeting continued. Mr. Roy Friedman's old dog took the floor.

· 28 ·

THE old dog came forward and took a place at the doorman's feet. He glanced around the room and spoke in these words:

"Dear friends, it has been very difficult for me to listen patiently to the various proposals presented so far at this meeting. Up to now the conclusions, in my opinion, are all the same. Those who have already spoken wish to distance themselves from human beings, or at least become independent of them, even to the point, if possible, of turning them into slaves. And most of you have spoken about the ordeals you've been through and the abuse you have suffered at the hands of human beings. It would not be out of order, I believe, for my relatives here to also present their grievances. Look at me, for example, see how old I look. I have chronic stomach disorders and my yellowed teeth are full of cavities because of the candies Mr. Friedman constantly feeds me. At least I have some of my teeth left, though in terrible condition; but look at my sisters who live in Dr. Joseph Rozeman's apartment. They are even worse off, because their own teeth were filed down and covered by false ones that are so large they can barely close their mouths. Impossible for them to show their distress; instead they have to smile forever. . . ."

"I also have artificial teeth," the bear broke in. "That's outrageous enough, but at least I don't have to smile all the time."

"That's because your thick upper lip can hide everything," asserted the dog. "Besides, I'm talking about our problems now, not yours; wait your turn. . . . Well, as I was saying, we all suffer hardships of one kind or another, imposed on us more or less capriciously, and more or less without pity, by humans. I cannot help mentioning, for example, the sad case of our five chihuahuas, who are forced to dance night and day at the whim of the super's son. . . . In short, human beings cause us a lot of grief. But, because of that, are we then going to deny the love they have shown us? I know, of course, that in our particular case, because of our great intelligence and talent, they are more affectionate with us than they are with other species. Anyway, we must come to an obvious conclusion: Separated from human beings, we are nothing. To abandon them is impossible. To ruin them, an absurd idea after all, would also ruin us. You are probably unaware, which is perfectly understandable (except for Mrs. Rat and Mr. Rabbit, who, by burrowing in the stacks of newspapers the Oscars keep, should be better informed), you are probably unaware, as I said, of what is happening with some animal species that for many generations have lived completely apart from man. Well, incredible as it may seem, they are trying to move closer to humans. Have you noticed how blue herons, creatures of the wild, now live very near cities? And something even more incredible: whales, who up to now have lived among icebergs and as far away from humans as possible, have recently been swimming up to boats, trying to ingratiate themselves and communicate with their most relentless enemies, humans, in a language that to them is nothing but a deep moan. . . . Do we consider ourselves stronger than whales or faster than blue herons? Are we so conceited, can we put on such airs, as to think we could survive far away from human beings? Instead of separation, I am proposing quite the opposite: rapprochement and negotiation leading to an agreement with goodwill on both sides, as it should be. Human beings are neither better nor worse than we are, but they can be worse because they are more powerful, and they can be better because they are more intelligent. . . . Understanding, obedience, affection are what we need to offer, since they are stronger than we are and our own survival depends on our behavior."

We don't know exactly whether the old dog intended to end his proposal at this point, but protests from the fish, the rat, the bear, the turtle, and particularly Brenda Hill's cat (who was meowing furiously) would not have let him continue, though for the record we must report that the chihuahuas were wagging their tails and dancing in support of Mr. Friedman's dog. Regardless, Cleopatra did not take sides, and yet probably to pacify the feline — who definitely wanted to pounce on the dog — she gave the floor to the cat.

29

OUR friend the dog," the cat began, "considers himself very sophisticated, and of course to him we are just a bunch of troublemakers. However, with all his culture, it seems he has not read his master's most popular book over the ages, the Bible. Well, in the Apocalypse we can read, and I quote exactly: 'Outside are the dogs and the murderers,' that is, outside the gates of heaven, dogs and humans: for as far as I know, the word *murderers* applies only to humans. So, if we follow the precepts of this work of man, which we could rightly call canonic, a work supposedly written by a superior being that called himself God, then we see that this superior being concludes, perhaps because he truly is God, that human beings and dogs should be banished from the face of the earth. Therefore, if we follow what the Bible says, we should proceed immediately to expel the man and the dog from this gathering."

Having said this, the cat pounced on Mr. Friedman's dog with such violence that only thanks to the quick intervention of the bear, the ape, and Cleopatra herself, was tragedy averted. Realizing it was thus impossible to continue her attack, the cat sprang up on the doorman's chest, and taking advantage of the fact that he couldn't defend himself (he still had the fishbowl in his hands), tore his uniform and then clawed his face. Only the swift talons of John Lockpez's parrots and the acrobatic leaps of the ape saved the doorman from being seriously hurt.

Restrained by the parrots and the ape, and Cleopatra's glare, the cat gradually quieted down, though she couldn't hold back a furious meow when the dog claimed his right to defend himself and added the following:

"What Mrs. Cat said is nothing but her usual nonsense. How could humans be so self-defeating as to banish themselves and their best friends at the same time? If the Bible separates dogs and men, it is not for twisted or discriminatory reasons, it is just a matter of rank. The dog's favor with God is obvious. So much so that even when God created the English language (just as He created everything else), as a symbol of divinity, He determined that His name in English, GOD, would be, if read backwards, DOG; and DOG would be, if read backwards, GOD. This revelation seems to indicate that *God* and *dog* are one and the same. . . . In fact it's easy to reach the conclusion that the dog is God disguised as a dog to be always close to man. And in this way, undetected and with great humility, *He* is always able to protect him."

Before other animals could launch an attack on the dog, in a climate of terrible tension, Cleopatra gave the floor to the squirrel.

30

THOUGH the squirrel addressed the assembly in human language, she spoke so quickly that only through the notes our doorman wrote afterward were we able to know exactly what the animal said. First of all, she reproached the dog for his subservience to mankind and said that if the whale or the blue heron had any reason to approach humans, that reason should be investigated; for if it's true that they were attracted by human superiority, the opposite could also be true; that is, they recognized in humans a weakness, a suicidal bent, which their ancestral reverence for life urged them to correct. . . .

In the specific case of the whale, the squirrel added, it was too much to say that whales could consider themselves weaker than humans, when even she considered herself, despite her diminutive size compared to a whale, a thousand times more agile than a human being. And in order to prove it, she began leaping around swiftly over the heads of all the other members of the assembly. Finally, hanging by her tail from an electric cable that stretched across the basement, she continued her speech in that upside-down position. She asserted that all animals ought to keep a position independent of humans, even though it wasn't necessary to declare open war, which, besides being costly, would be extremely dangerous. "What's more," she ended up saying, still swinging by her tail and looking with her large, bulging eyes at the audience, who craned their necks and listened, "I would propose to keep diplomatic relations with humans, so long as these do not compromise our freedom." And then, perhaps to demonstrate what freedom meant to her, the squirrel let go of the cable and flew through the air, landing on a heating pipe at the other end of the basement. The whole group got up to follow the squirrel. But since the pipe was practically red-hot, the squirrel let out a squeal and took a great leap onto an old discarded motor. They reassembled in a circle around her while she went on to say that the dog's unconditional submissiveness was abominable, and so was the cat's arrogance and her rigid intolerance of humans. "This intolerance is more talk than action," she said, eyeing the cat, "because, after all, even though people say cats close their eyes so as not to see the humans who feed them, the truth is they gladly accept room and board from humans. Anyway, the animal that most resembles the cat is the dog. And as far as this feline specimen is concerned, the one who lives in Brenda Hill's apartment, I can only say that her submission to her mistress is despicable. Look at her!" The squirrel then stood high on her hind legs, and addressing the whole audience, pointed at the cat. "There she is, all covered with her mistress's ribbons and bows. If this cat so despises human beings, why on earth does she allow herself to be pampered and humiliated in this way? I bet her rear end is even perfumed. . . . And now I ask you, when have you seen squirrels with colored ribbons or necklaces hanging from their necks? *That* we leave for cats and dogs. . . . And as for both the cat's and the dog's theories about the supposed relationship between God and the matters under discussion, I think they are bizarre and out of place. First of all, we are not here to talk about theology, but to find a practical solution to our material concerns; secondly, the Bible, which I myself have also skipped through, is a product of mankind and therefore not something we have to include in our beliefs or way of life; and thirdly, though in English *God* is *dog* spelled backwards, English was not the language used by the writers of the Bible, nor was it the one spoken by the god in it. I am therefore, like the doorman (whom I have watched for months from my tree), all in favor of maintaining our freedom while at the same time keeping a friendly relationship with humans. We don't have to be subservient to them, as the dog says, but we don't have to claw furiously at their faces either, the way the cat (who is as hysterical as her mistress) just did. I think we can peacefully watch people from the treetops while we munch on a tasty nut. I realize that some of my distant cousins don't have the same ability as squirrels to climb tall trees and observe things from above. I'm referring, of course, to the poor rat, who must be content with what people leave lying around. . . ."

When the squirrel said this, the rat squeaked in protest, and without asking for Cleopatra's permission, cried out that she wanted to know who had said that she, the rat, could not climb up as high as she pleased. Then, standing on her hind legs, and addressing the squirrel, she said:

"You are nothing but a rat with a disproportionate tail and bug eyes. In fact, you are nothing but a rat who pretends to be a monkey and that's the reason why you go around swinging from one branch to another. . . ."

This last statement yet again offended the orangutan, who stood half-mockingly in front of the rat. Just as he was about to give a response, his sixth sense (or rather, his sense of smell) perceived that an outsider was approaching, and he immediately reported this to the assembly.

"They are a man and a woman, and they are about a hundred feet away," said the snake with absolute certainty. Cleopatra confirmed the news and adjourned the meeting until the following day at six in the evening, when the doorman had his break.

The Egyptian dog asked everybody to leave quietly through the door leading to the inner courtyard. But the news of the two humans approaching created panic among the animals. They were terribly afraid of being punished, and some, like the snake and the rat, of actually being exterminated. In spite of Cleopatra's calm instructions, chaos ruled in the basement. The bear, almost too big for the door to the garden, insisted on being one of the first to escape. He thought the woman approaching was, without a doubt, Cassandra Levinson, and she would punish him in a way that only he knew. The ape, who had lately been hiding out in the empty attic at the Warrems' penthouse, shrieked out of fear of losing his living quarters and being sent to some zoo. The five chihuahuas were whimpering and adjusting their portable radios, and meanwhile the parrots, flying above all the other animals, were causing a great commotion. The turtles didn't have a chance: by the time the super along with Brenda Hill materialized in the basement, they had barely crawled six feet. . . . At the sight of Brenda Hill, the cat, fearing for her life, let out a pathetic meow and, strange as it seems, tried to hide at the feet of the doorman, who, not knowing what else to do, was still holding the fishbowl.

Thus, Juan suddenly found himself with Brenda Hill's cat between his feet and Mr. Lockpez's golden fish in the fishbowl in his hands. As if all of this weren't enough, the two linked turtles were going around him in a circle, while the other animals did their best to escape.

WHAT have you done to my poor little kitty!"
cried Brenda Hill to the doorman.

When the cat heard the one she feared would be her executioner call her "kitty," she meowed and moaned even more pathetically than before, and fled from the doorman's feet to rub against her mistress's skinny ankles.

Brenda Hill took the cat in her arms as if it were a child miraculously rescued from under the wheels of a moving train, and looking at the doorman as if *he* were the murderous train, she said:

"What right do you think you have to dare bring my kitty down here? What were you doing with her?"

"Madam," the super said then, "this is burglary. This man not only broke into your apartment and took your cat, but he also stole the fish and the turtles from Mr. Lockpez."

"That is not true," said Juan, intending to argue that he had found the animals out in the garden, and had locked them in the basement in order to notify their owners. But how could he explain the golden fish getting away, sneaking out of their apartment, fishbowl and all? And if he told the truth, which he wasn't going to do, he would have to betray his new friends, particularly Cleopatra; besides, no one would believe him, and they would still consider him not only a thief but also shameless and crazy. He had to accept the grave and obvious facts: there he was, holding in his hands the fishbowl with Mr. Lockpez's two golden fish. The super provided, with relish, the only logical explanation: the doorman had broken into the apartments of Mr. Lockpez and Brenda Hill and he had stolen the animals. *"Forced entry and robbery"*—the super envisioned himself declaring to the jury that he now understood how other valuable objects had mysteriously disappeared from the building. And he ran through a mental list of things he himself had stolen that he could now blame on the doorman: three plastic brooms, six gallons of industrial-strength cleaning solution, a drum of oil, several dozen light bulbs . . . The super was sorry he had not brought the pair of handcuffs he kept in his apartment, obviously without legal authority, in case he had to arrest somebody.

"I'll call the police right away," he told Brenda Hill, who started out ahead of him; and turning to the doorman, he advised him not to run away because it would make things much worse for him.

The super decided to lock up Juan in the closet of the lobby until the patrol car got there.

"Thank goodness you knew how to defend yourself," Brenda Hill cooed to her cat as she straightened her ribbons and bows. And she observed with pride the scratches her cat had left on the doorman's face.

"She was the one that gave the alarm," the super confirmed. "It was thanks to her loud meows that I was able to discover the thief."

In solemn procession, the three of them went up the stairs and into the lobby. Brenda Hill with her cat, the doorman with the fishbowl, and the super with the two turtles.

"I hope he has not raped her," Mrs. Hill moaned.

"Rape? Rape who?" questioned the super, rather confused.

"My cat! These people are capable of anything."

"Yes, ma'am," agreed the super, locking the doorman in the closet.

"You should press charges against him for bestiality!" piped in Mrs. Pietri, who had just found out what the commotion was about and was getting ready to inform everybody in the building.

"Well, you should also tell the police about the rape," the super advised Brenda Hill.

"Call me as soon as they arrive," she responded and, with an air of offended royalty, took the elevator.

The super tried repeatedly to contact the nearest police station, but nobody answered; he called another precinct, and the line was always busy. Finally, in desperation, he called the general emergency number for New York City.

Mr. Pietri had finally reached the police when the elevator door opened and Cleopatra and Mr. Stephen Warrem stepped out. Mrs. Pietri's efficient information service had already reached him, as well as the other tenants in the building. With a gesture, Mr. Warrem ordered the super to hang up.

"It was a robbery," said the super.

"We don't know yet," answered Mr. Warrem.

"Then how did the doorman manage to get hold of Mr. Lockpez's turtles and golden fish, and Mrs. Brenda Hill's cat?"

"We don't know yet," Mr. Warrem said again.

"The police will have to investigate," insisted the super.

"When the time comes, they may be of help," answered Mr. Warrem. "But listen to me for a second: Mr. Lockpez lives on the twenty-fifth floor, isn't that right? He has been home all morning and his door was locked from the inside, he told me just now. There is only one window that opens onto the street, and from there, on the twenty-fifth floor, the doorman would have had to jump with a fishbowl full of water in one hand and two live turtles in the other. Do you actually think that he could have accomplished such a feat?"

"What counts is that we caught him red-handed with the turtles and the fish."

"They were in the basement, which you, as superintendent, ought to be watching more carefully. . . . Some of the neighbors are complaining that their pets also escaped and have just now returned. And, as for me, something incredible has happened: Cleopatra got out on her own and came back, but tapes from the video monitors show that nobody even tried to approach the area."

"A dog, sir, can come in and out pretty easily, but fish in a fishbowl?"

"True," Mr. Warrem said almost paternally, "but the problem, as you can see, is more complex, and if the police should intervene, they would get in the way. Look, for the time being let me and my friends take care of this. And don't worry, we won't let the doorman get away."

"Of course not, as long as I still have him locked up."

"Let him out. And as I said, leave this to me and my friends. Oh, and please, first check with me, before you do anything." And as Mr. Warrem was leaving, with a gesture that was so casual as to be almost imperceptible, he slipped into the super's hand a $100 bill.

· 32 ·

THE super realized he had to free the doorman. And though he could not notify the authorities until he received orders from Mr. Warrem (who, according to Mrs. Pietri, was a close friend of the New York City Chief of Police), he could, at least, start a general campaign against the doorman among the tenants so that they would, by consensus, get him fired from his post, even if Mr. Warrem was against it for reasons the super could not understand.

We feel it is necessary, for truth's sake, to include in this document those very reasons that the super simply could not understand because he did not know them.

The specialists Mr. Warrem had hired to investigate the strange relationship between Cleopatra and the doorman had not yet reached any satisfactory conclusions. They insisted that, for the benefit of their investigation, the doorman must remain free to act. And as for Cleopatra, one almost insurmountable obstacle prevented them from keeping her under stricter surveillance, and that was her extremely keen sense of smell. Knowing that the animal had had two mysterious encounters with the doorman in the basement, they decided to rig the place with a supersensitive system of hidden recorders and video cameras, which were monitored, of course, from Mr. Warrem's strategically located offices, where Cleopatra had no access. At home, the Warrems pretended not to notice Cleopatra's escapades. Meanwhile, our doorman returned that same afternoon to his usual post by the big glass door.

* * *

I T seems almost unnecessary for us to record here the concerns that were overwhelming our doorman at this point.

Now, he began thinking, or even saying aloud to himself, not only did the salvation of all the people in the building depend upon him, but also the salvation of all the animals. The fact that Cleopatra herself had invited him to participate in their assembly indicated (as has been mentioned) that in the end they had to reach an agreement, and he, the doorman, would have to approve it or veto it. . . . Besides, after the rest of the animals had their say (there were still four more to go), he, the doorman, would have to speak too; and his speech about salvation would have to be new even to him, since it would not be addressed to human beings as before. *But I can't forget those human beings either, I am one of them,* he would tell himself. Again he would begin to pace the lobby, muttering to himself and gesturing nervously.

Our doorman's situation was indeed a very difficult one and his psychological state verged on desperation, as all the tenants would confirm later. The situation demanded from him a total change of perspective; as if suddenly he were being forced to abandon a distraught world that he loved nevertheless, and move to an unknown and, literally, *inhuman* realm that seemed to offer no promise of salvation. And above all, "and this is the most serious problem for me," he told himself, it was not that he had to choose one desperate situation over the other and try to find a solution, but that he had to take on both sides, each excluding the other. And all too soon he would be separated by force from both groups: he would not even be able to listen to them, let alone save them. Already the tenants were avoiding him when they entered or left the building. They would rush past him, looking at him apprehensively out of the corners of their eyes, and they even suspected something dangerous lurking in his extreme politeness. This could not go on, of course; after all, they were the owners of the building and would not tolerate this situation much longer.

The doorman was feeling overwhelmed by the uncertainty

of his situation when yet another event, seemingly incredible, occurred that same evening.

As Mr. Warrem was leaving the building with Cleopatra for their usual walk, the dog suddenly used her teeth to snatch the book Juan was trying to read. After a quick look at the text the animal viciously tore it to shreds. Then, regaining her usual regal composure, she stalked out. Mr. Warrem, who had been watching the scene, was flabbergasted and asked the doorman for the title of the book he was reading. This information was vital for the specialists studying the case.

"It was *Being and Nothingness*, sir, by Sartre, and in Spanish," answered Juan, apologetically.

"Don't worry, I'll get you another copy; but, please, read it at home," he said, and silently followed after Cleopatra.

Besides the anxiety he felt already, a new kind of desperation took hold of our doorman when Miss Scarlett Reynolds, back from her walk, for the first time refrained from greeting him and, what was more unbelievable, didn't ask him for money. . . . Always looking much older than she really was, she now assumed the airs of an offended grand duchess as she crossed the lobby dragging her rag dog — which had become for her like a royal train — and disappeared into the elevator.

Juan desperately needed to listen to someone, to have somebody confide their problems to him. But for that he would have to wait until the next risky meeting with the animals on the following evening.

And as he thought of the animals, the image of the Great Door came back to him, though by now he didn't know who should be the first to go through it.

WHEN Cleopatra announced that, with the order she had established, the next speaker would be the rabbit, there was a moment of confusion in the assembly. Instead of stepping to the center of the gathering as the others had done, the rabbit fearfully backed away and hid in the thick fur of the bear.

Thanks to some skillful maneuvers by the squirrel and the cat (now without any bows around her neck), the rabbit finally came out of his improvised hiding place, still racked by spasmodic shivers, and under the half-protective, half-threatening gaze of Cleopatra, he began to speak.

"I'm frightened, really, really frightened," he whimpered. "In fact, I'm scared to death. Yes, I'm so terrified I'm almost dead. But I'm also sure of one thing, that if it weren't for this fear, I wouldn't be half-dead, I'd be completely dead. That is, I would have killed myself, because fear is the only thing that keeps us alive. The meaning of life is based on nothing but fear. We fear death because death is nothing but a strong fear, something like the Great Fear, the Fear of Fears. Ah, what would become of us without fear! What are brave heroes made of, but fear? Fear cannot, however, be directed against a specific enemy: it has to extend over everything. A stone rolls and kills us; someone fires a gun, and it's me who gets shot; a wolf comes by and devours me; a car passes by and runs over me; I eat a poisonous plant by mistake and I drop dead; I get lost in the desert and I die of thirst; unawares, I scoot into a hole with no exit and I suffocate; I fall down a well and I drown; I am prey to the hawk in broad daylight, and at night the owl is after me. Fear! Fear! Fear! The walls of the world are made of fear. . . . And what is saddest of all is that the world exists because fear exists. . . . The world, being the way it is, is nothing but a zone of terror. And whoever fails to see it that way, perishes. Everything conspires against us. Everyone is our enemy. And, at the same time, everything conspires against everything else. So we are the enemies of everything. In such a world, and this is the only world there is, we are saved by mistrust, which is to say, by fear. It is the cowards who save themselves." For a moment the rabbit had to stop talking, his body shaken by opposing waves of independent shivers; that is, different parts of his body were shaking on their own, as if fear itself did not allow his body to quake in an organized way. For instance, one foot would shiver in a direction opposite to the other; his stomach would at the same time cave in and protrude; one eye would keep blinking while the other one remained staring as if petrified; an ear would turn in every possible direction, while the other one, straight up, pointed at the ceiling. Finally, with a great effort, he pulled himself together and continued his speech, though every once in a while he hopped, he squealed, and often glanced out of the corners of his eyes all around the room. "What we are doing here is very dangerous. Just to be here is extremely dangerous. The doorman knows this as well as I do, and he is shaking too, just like me or even more. Whether you can see it or not is another matter; I see it because fear makes me see everything very clearly. This meeting is actually a trap. We have surely been brought here to be 'hunted like rabbits,' if I may use an expression that is so painfully familiar. Wouldn't it be better to go back right now to our own places? Or maybe to start running in any direction? Who is who in here? Nobody knows. Oh, God, let's quickly look for a place where we can dig a lot of holes! Wherever we go, let's burrow, burrow, burrow! Let's get into one hole at night, and leave it on the run the next day. Let's keep digging holes, more and more holes! Of course, digging holes can also be very dangerous. We can encounter all sorts of underground creatures always ready to eat us up. And once inside the hole, aren't we virtual prisoners? If anyone should block the opening, there would be no way out and we would perish. You have to be very careful, very careful, extremely careful. You have to keep your eyes wide open, your ears perked up, your feet ready to jump down into the hole or to stampede if necessary. . . . So what do we do then? Can you perhaps live without fear? And if we lose our fear, what is left? If we lose our fear, what will save us? I'm frightened, really, really frightened. I'm scared to death. Please, let's begin to burrow, burrow, burrow. . . . Because, don't forget, in life everything comes down to this: we have to be able to hide ourselves in a hole. And in this I'm sure the doorman supports me. What's more, I could even bet (if I weren't so afraid of controversy) that the doorman and I are the same thing (human or animal, I'd be scared to say). But what does he do but run from one hole into another? What do all people do but keep digging different holes, fixing their holes, coming out of holes, and getting into holes? Holes that subdivide into many more holes, into thousands of smaller holes. Holes to sleep, to bathe in, holes to keep your clothes, holes to store your food, holes to hide your jewels or keep your money safe . . . Holes undoubtedly created by fear. Look at their cities: holes multiplied endlessly by fear. Holes with bells and alarm systems, with protective wiring, policemen, and doormen. Our doorman is a doorman of holes. Our doorman is a doorman of Fear. If fear did not exist, why would doormen need to exist? But the doorman exists and I exist (that's obvious, isn't it?), and if we exist it is because fear exists, and because of it, we both want to have our own hole, a safe hole, as safe as it can be, of course, because nothing is totally safe. . . . But a hole, a hole, a hole where, even scared to death, we could take refuge sometimes. . . . And don't you know how to dig a hole? If you don't, you are lost. If you only have your fear, and no hole in which to hide, there is no escape for you. . . . In all truth, I think there is no escape, even though you have your hole. But let us dig holes, let's start to burrow, burrow, burrow! Right now!"

Here the rabbit, still shaking, wanted to make a practical demonstration of how to dig holes, but his teeth and his nails were useless against the cement of the basement floor.

The rabbit screamed in terror.

"You see," he said, seemingly on the brink of a heart attack, "we have been trapped. This is nothing but a cage. We are trapped! I'm terrified!"

And emitting an even louder shriek, he ran to hide himself in the bear's fur.

But the bear, whose turn it was to speak, stood up and pushed him away. Then the rabbit panicked and began screaming, begging not to be killed: he would take back everything he had said, he wanted them to forget everything, he didn't really mean it, and he had often lied; he would do anything in return if they didn't chop his head off right away and would let him leave now. But as nobody paid any attention to him, the rabbit interpreted their attitude as a conspiracy to murder him. More terrified than ever by this, he climbed up the doorman's legs and hid inside his jacket. And he squealed when the doorman petted him. But the doorman kept stroking his fur until the rabbit finally calmed down and summoned enough courage to stick his head out and say:

"As you see, the doorman and I are in agreement."

But right away, scared by the possible consequences of what he had just said, he disappeared again inside Juan's uniform.

34

WHEN the bear started to speak in the cold basement, the fly, who was next, was still fluttering around his snout to keep herself warm in the stream of his breath.

"First of all," the bear began, "I would like to make clear, just in case you were not aware of it, that my true color is not black. I am a polar bear. One of the many humiliations I've had to suffer (which out of respect for this meeting I won't go into) was to have my fur dyed black by my mistress, Mrs. Levinson, with whom, ugh!, I have been forced to fornicate." Here the bear shuddered in disgust, and then covered his eyes with his paws in shame. "I am a decent bear, and I find it abhorrent to have any kind of sexual contact except with my own kind. Besides, Mrs. Levinson's body is disgusting, full of old-age spots, freckles, varicose veins . . ."

"Oh, come on, don't pretend to be so innocent," interrupted the squirrel ironically. "From the trees I've seen you constantly looking at the bottoms of women walking down the street."

"That's a lie!" protested the bear, "I watch the street just like any prisoner does, trying to escape, if only in my imagination. However, I'm not here to talk about my personal grievances, but about how to solve our common problems. I must confess that the idea of digging holes proposed by our friend the rabbit attracts me, as I'm sure it attracts our doorman. I was absolutely fascinated by this idea. Now, the hole where we would live should be large and nice, not a temporary, makeshift hideout. No, sir, we won't be intimidated. We want to withdraw to a world of our own, I agree, where we won't feel persecuted, harassed, or even bothered by human beings, who are always changing things for the worse; the farther away we get from them, the better it will be for us, since *sublata causa, tollitur effectus*. . . . I like the idea of a hole, yes, but like a lion's den, a hidden fortress. Our cause should be an invulnerable bastion," he said, very proud of his strong rhetoric, inflated like his voluminous body. "And where should we build our citadel?" he continued, savoring his words. "Well, as I have indirectly suggested, at the North Pole. . . . And why? Simply because in a cold climate our food will not spoil (and one of our chief purposes is to eat); we won't have to suffer the debilitating diseases of warmer climates that could decimate us (and one of our main purposes is to have a healthy life); and we won't be bothered by the incessant noise in every other part of the globe (and one of our main purposes is to rest); in other words, careless human beings will no longer inconvenience us. Besides, we could hibernate, that is, sleep and dream to our hearts' content, and therefore our minds would become brighter and brighter, as in my case, and our bodies healthier and healthier, like mine. And I don't need to emphasize that vim and vigor, as well as health, are indispensable in order to enjoy our freedom, though *stultorum infinitus est numerus*. . . . After all, what is freedom when your body is weak and racked by all sorts of diseases? Freedom would become as meaningless and loathsome as life itself under those conditions. Longevity, as our friend the turtle said, is priceless if you can enjoy your freedom; otherwise it is a humiliation. And on the question of longevity I'm sure our doorman agrees with me, because human beings, with few exceptions, want to live a long life, even longer than is reasonable. They even want to outlive themselves, to pass on to us so much nonsense before they succumb. *Vae soli.*"

35

LOWERING his snout in a solemn gesture, the bear brought his speech to an end. The fly, always hovering in his breath so as not to perish, began to speak.

"My dear friends," and she landed briefly on the bear's nose, "or should I also say 'dear enemies,' to include everyone? I risked my life because of the cold to attend this meeting. Was my motion left almost for last perhaps in the hope I would die before speaking?" Here she flew away dangerously far, quickly coming back and landing on the bear's brow, where for a moment she rubbed her legs over her wings and then continued: "Anyway, I've never minded much the idea of dying. I don't exactly agree with the bear (I hope this will not make him hold his breath now), nor with the turtle, the rabbit, or most of the others gathered here, who are bent on living as long as possible, under any conditions. No, my dear friends (or enemies?). What is the sense of having a long life if it's ruled by fear? What is the sense of prolonging your life when you are imprisoned and terrified, not daring to stick your head out of your hole or stop licking the hand that feeds you crumbs and scraps, or takes you out with a collar around your neck, or locks you up in a cage? And mind you, this is in the best of cases. . . . Isn't it better to enjoy life fully for an instant and then die? Do you honestly think that something not worth dying for could be worth living for? Look at me, here and now, in this freezing temperature: Am I not risking my life for the thrill of being with you in these decisive moments of our lives? The bear would only need to hold his breath for a moment, and I would freeze to death; or you, any of you, could open your mouth wide and swallow me, as our friends here, the dogs and the lizards, have been doing for centuries. . . . Don't you think I have considered all of these imminent dangers? It's also because of them, for the thrill of risking my life, that I'm here with you. Yes, I know you may think I am also possessed by a sick urge for self-destruction like Miss Avilés. Quite the contrary. Life, for her, had no meaning, so she was always seeking death, while for me life is so rich that the price of death is insignificant compared to the joy of really being alive for a minute. This is my motto: live to the hilt (and thus always in danger) for a second, or two or three if possible, and then perish. To soar, while still strong, upon a warm ray of sunlight and then, still entranced, to fall. To go in an instant, without even realizing it, from ecstasy into eternal sleep. But before that, to have experienced the intense joys of filth or of cake, of milk or urine, of blood or wine . . . So it's not a matter of escaping or not escaping, but of how to flutter around with joy before vanishing forever, and even to see that final moment as one to be savored. . . . But I understand that one can do very little while imprisoned. And the doorman also understands this: I have seen him fluttering about almost like me, but without the skill, within his glass cage. . . . Thank you very much, dear friends and enemies, for listening. I hope you have understood my message."

Just then, the ape, who had been jumping around, opened one of the basement windows and let in an icy gust of wind. The fly then rushed into the bear's mouth, begging not to be swallowed.

"To be honest, we have not understood you very well," said the ape to the fly, snickering sarcastically, and he closed the window again in order to begin his speech.

36

So many serious things have been said in this meeting," began the ape half-jokingly, "so serious it's impossible to take them seriously, since that would show a lack of seriousness on our part. . . . Life has been discussed here and, of course, the new kind of life it seems all of us wish to have. The most vital issue, however, has not been considered: we have not yet asked ourselves what is the true, deep meaning of life. Life, dear friends, is nothing more, and nothing less, than a game. The way we animals play it is a clean game, if cruel at times, but we know what to expect from everyone. However, for human beings (whom you, to your disgrace, are trying to emulate instead of letting them imitate us), life has become a dirty game and, what is worse, that game has been taken so seriously that it has changed from a game to something oppressive; so oppressive that people don't even know what freedom is, much less how to enjoy it. What is freedom, then, if not the chance to play, to have and make fun, even of ourselves, and to try to understand others a little better even while we mimic and make fun of them? And that's the way it has to be, since no being is quite that different or original, but a sort of imitation of many others. Aren't the eyes of the rattlesnake like those of the parrot? Doesn't the parrot have the tongue of a woman? And doesn't the woman smell like a fish and have the nails of a cat? Doesn't the cat have the ears of a rabbit? And doesn't the rabbit jitter like a chicken? Doesn't the chicken lay eggs like the turtle, the duck, and the platypus? And doesn't the platypus have a bill like a duck and the shape of a porcupine? And isn't the porcupine as gruff as people? And don't people want to fly like doves, swim like ducks, and dig tunnels like rabbits? . . . So we come to see that the only way to be is to be a little bit like somebody else, or something else, to be more precise. We are truer to our own natures if we keep changing. Let's walk on all fours, and then on one leg, on two, and on none! Let's run! Let's hop! Let's fly! Let's crawl! Our true identity is a constant disguise, an eternal joke. The only truly serious thing is death. Let's mistrust serious faces; they have been wearing a mask for so long they can't take it off. This is another difference between animals and humans: we don't wear masks, we *are*. They, in order *to be*, have to live in a perpetual struggle to prove what they are. In the game that is life, they always lose because they are tainted with hypocrisy. They have broken the rules of the great carnival. They don't act out of mischief, but out of mean pettiness. They are not fun-loving, never have been, but murderous, and worse yet, they are spoilsports, cretins, too self-important and pompous. And when we try to show them how they really are, behind their masks, they call us monkeys, apes, orangutans, gorillas, or something like that. . . . And when, pathetically, they imitate us, they excuse themselves by saying that we are the ones who imitate them. Humans believe and insanely proclaim they are the measure of everything. But we know that each thing has its own measure, and that this measure is also flexible and changing. . . . The fly's position agrees with mine insofar as jumping, dancing, and enjoying life is concerned, but I find in her a spirit of guilt, of sacrifice (no doubt copied from humans, since she is always around them), that I reject. There is no reason to pay for an ephemeral pleasure with an early death. On the contrary, pleasure should last and drive death away. . . . Let's understand reality at its deepest level, that is, as it really is. Let's laugh at everything, let's be versatile, irreverent, and light-hearted. In that sense, the doorman is my best ally. He behaves differently with each tenant; he is what each tenant wants him to be, but at the same time, he wants all the tenants to be what he would like them to be. In this way, he is constantly wrestling between contradictory attitudes. Notice, for example, that he is a doorman and he also writes; but he writes and does not publish, in contrast to the real writers, who publish but do not write. So our doorman is the embodiment of parody. And I am sure he is our guest of honor because of this. Yes, he is our guest of honor because he represents the supreme parody. But, dear friends, if you have lost the spirit of playfulness and the ability to laugh at yourselves as well as at others, there is no point in continuing this session. After all, play is the only measure of all things. And if we distance ourselves from the human race, we shouldn't hate it, we should be able to make fun of it more freely."

At this moment, the orangutan interrupted his speech and began imitating different types of people. Right before his audience, he transformed himself into a young streetwalker, a decorated civil servant, a saint transfixed in meditation, a hunchbacked old woman, a medieval queen, a famous movie actor, a flamboyant gay man, a newborn babe kicking and screaming (and here the orangutan, to add a bit of realism to his act, peed all over his audience), a classical ballerina, the Holy Father saying mass in the Vatican, a middle-aged nymphomaniac in whom everyone quickly recognized Brenda Hill, and then Miss Hill's cat (and he imitated her meowing very well), Mr. Pietri, Cassandra Levinson, some kind of monkey, our doorman, the solemn bear standing next to him, and the noisy parrot, who got all excited and, in a gesture of gratitude, perched herself on the ape's head and began an exact voice-over of the characters the ape kept on imitating.

By now, the audience was enthralled. Those who could, applauded; those who couldn't, bellowed, warbled, grunted, hissed, barked, or squawked. . . . In the euphoria of his success, the ape opened the door and walked out to the interior courtyard, trailed by the entire retinue, and, with the parrot's help, he began imitating the rest of the tenants in the building. It was quite a spectacle to see all the animals parading in the snow against the winter twilight, warmed by their own breath, and surrounding the ape and the doorman, who was hopelessly trying to stop the procession. For a moment, Juan expected a cue from Cleopatra's violet gaze, but her intense, enigmatic look told him nothing. The clamor of the animals in unison assumed a pulsing momentum. The snake was shaking its rattles louder and louder and the turtle was trying to stand on his hind legs on the ice. Suddenly, in the middle of that pandemonium, the orangutan, shrieking wildly, grabbed the doorman's hands, and before Juan knew it, the ape was leading him in a bizarre dance.

At that moment, most of the windows in the building were flung open, one by one, and in spite of the intense cold, the astonished residents stuck out their heads. When Brenda Hill saw her beloved cat in the company of that carnival rabble, a piercing scream escaped from her lips. John Lockpez, scandalized, intoned a prayer together with his family. Cassandra Levinson pronounced her loud condemnation of capitalism and the alienation it produced, and the two Oscars added a few high-pitched operatic howls while Scarlett Reynolds, planning to sue the management of the building and even the city, collapsed, pretending to faint. Then Mr. Pietri took his old double-barreled shotgun and fired several shots in the air while his wife looked for Mr. Warrem, whom she held ultimately responsible because he had protected the doorman.

"Madam, we have already called for an ambulance," replied Mr. Warrem at the door, without inviting her in.

"But isn't it better also to call the police? He's a dangerous crazy man! See what he has done to the animals!"

"No," said Mr. Warrem, and closed the door. And so Mrs. Pietri could not find out whether that "no" meant they should not call the police, or that the doorman was not a dangerous madman, as she thought he was, who had driven the animals crazy.

T HE paramedic emergency team came prepared for violence, but they did not have to resort to their professional knowledge of judo. Juan offered no resistance when they led him to the ambulance and drove him to the city's mental hospital. The staff psychiatrists, encouraged by the detectives, veterinarians, and doctors all acting under Mr. Warrem's orders, tried desperately to determine what sort of madness had possessed our doorman. Since they could not discover any clues, they certified that he was seriously ill and, with the help of tape recordings and even some videotapes made in the basement by Mr. Warrem's detectives, diagnosed his case as "magnetic ventriloquism." They explained it as a new and terrible disease that causes its victims to believe they are "talking animals" and then behave accordingly. In Juan's case, the doctors observed, the disorder was complicated by the fact that he did not think of himself as any animal in particular, but that, according to the taped evidence, he would constantly switch identities, sometimes assuming the personality of a parrot, a bear, or a turtle, and even that of a fly. What completely baffled the physicians, and Mr. Warrem's detectives as well, was the variety of vocal registers the doorman had at his command, all without using his lips — that is, using his diaphragm only, as the clandestine videotapes taken during the strange meeting proved beyond any doubt.

The most puzzling thing about this disorder was that, once the patient had been admitted to the clinic, all the symptoms disappeared. The doorman no longer thought of himself as a parrot or an ape, and neither did he attempt to be the spokesperson for any of those creatures. Finally, the psychiatrists decided that it would be a good idea to bring to the hospital those animals the doorman had "magnetized," and to observe how the madman and the animals reacted to the encounter. But when they informed Mr. Warrem, he refused to even consider it.

The truth was that after listening to the tape recordings and studying the videotapes, besides having witnessed the scene in the garden with the doorman and all the animals, Mr. Warrem had decided to keep Cleopatra as far away from Juan as possible. On the other hand, and we think it is only fair to add here (also considering the exorbitant amount we had to pay for this bit of information: a thousand dollars to Mr. Warrem's private secretary), Stephen Warrem was none too sure about the doorman's so-called "magnetic ventriloquism." He contended, with acute perception, that "those recorded animal voices sounded human, but there was also something not quite human about them. . . ." Mr. Warrem did not truly know whether the doorman was speaking like the animals, or if the animals themselves had really spoken, but he was certain that the mystery here went beyond Juan's madness. In the meantime, Mr. Warrem embarked on a costly investigation of this new disorder, "magnetic ventriloquism," coming to the conclusion that there was no medical record of anything like it, not even remotely. Obviously it was so "new," as the hospital had insisted, that the doorman was its first victim. It would not be inaccurate to say that Mr. Warrem had practically lost all interest in the doctors' speculations.

For their part, the psychiatrists decided to continue their "animal experimentation with a clinical subject," and, even though they were not allowed to bring the animals to the clinic, they did bring numerous tape recordings of vocal sounds produced by the most diverse creatures. The therapeutic session consisted of having the doorman sit in a chair at the center of a white room, which was completely bare except for the electrodes and machines connected to the patient's head and to a monitor screen. After the room was hermetically sealed, various animal sounds would be heard: trills, hissing, barks, meows, snorts, bleats, buzzing; a veritable acoustic jungle filled the room. The sessions were intense, and the screen showed hundreds of complicated graphs to be minutely analyzed by the psychiatrists.

It was an incredible melange: an Andalusian horse would neigh, preceded by the mournful song of a dying whale; a string of melody from a Florida mockingbird would be followed by the groans of a Greenland walrus, and then by the mating noises of six Australian kangaroos. In the middle of all this, our doorman at times let his mind wander, and the images in these fantasies were so vivid that they became one more reality in the ever-changing repertory of realities that had been his life. In this way, Juan returned to the past. And what did he find? He found himself, thinner and younger, trying to get into his parents' house. That day the door had been bolted from the inside because his father, after much scheming and at considerable risk, had managed to get a nice chunk of pork from the black market, and Juan, the son, had been excluded from the family table. With his body against the door, his ear on the lock, he stood listening to them, his mother and father, as they savored that rare banquet with real passion. Not until they had finished the meal would he be able to throw himself into an armchair in the living room and go to sleep. . . . All he had left were the streets, which were being watched, and there was a risk in just walking around, particularly being young and having long hair — hair that, in a gesture of subconscious rebellion, he had refused to cut. . . . Back, farther back in his memory (but now he couldn't help hearing the hooting of two Caribbean owls while a Canadian moose bellowed), farther back in the past, a past that for us immigrants is always present, there is a young boy trying to sleep between his mother's legs, deep inside, deep inside, while she is beating him. . . . Later, later (a lion roars and a tiny cartacuba answers), later in time, in that past that for us doesn't exist because, like it or not, we always live in it, Juan sees himself in a rage, walking along the carefully patrolled beaches of his country, trying to find out, fearfully trying to find out how to get to the other side of the sea. And he saw himself in a gigantic blue balloon, taking off from the same roof of the collective building where he had lived, soaring in the sky forever, forever. Forever trying to escape from that place, where his whole childhood and early youth, his life, had been a frustrated attempt to be accepted somewhere besides the work camp, the compulsory military service, the obligatory hours of guard duty, the obligatory assemblies and meetings, the mass rallies, the official, irrevocable decree that he surrender the only thing he had, and which anyway he could not enjoy: his ephemeral, and therefore wonderful, youth. . . . *But I seek, but I seek, but I feel, but I shout* (and now he began speaking louder and louder, his voice mingling with the squawks of a Central American macaw and the bleating of a Sicilian goat), *I shout in the middle of the ocean, in the work camp, underwater, walking alongside the sun-baked Malecón, up in the trees or in the middle of traffic, inside the train or under the snow, above the palm trees or on the sand, forty days and forty nights, opening and closing the door, I am looking for a way out. And then we'll see, we'll see horses and elephants, we'll see skies and corridors, bubbling whirls, creeping vines, deserts, and the sign of the crab on the moon.* . . . At this point the psychiatrists looked at each other, weary-eyed, convinced that the doorman's madness would remain impenetrable. But after all, they said to console themselves by way of professional justification, wasn't all madness an enigma? And so they ended the session for the moment, silencing that portable jungle.

However, parts of Juan's rambling speech were pretty clear to us, and it is only fair to admit it. It all came out of the need, unavoidable for us immigrants, to go back to our own world (a need perhaps intensified in Juan's case by all of those cheeps, trills, bellows, and songs). We, too, in spite of our absence for so many years, never stop thinking of a hypothetical return. And at times it seems there is still a contact (an illusion, surely) or odd bits of news keep reaching us from that sinking world we abandoned: a long-forgotten friend just died under dubious circumstances, a distant relative (an old enemy) fell out of favor with the system, someone we had hated now inspires our pity. But all of this we see again and again as if through a dense fog, and when we come back to our senses and return once more to this place where we have been living for so many years, we cannot be sure if all these memories, even of hell itself, are fictions we cannot forget, or true events we cannot clearly remember. . . . Even the voices clamoring over there, even the applause of those who betray, and even the crackling of gunfire, and the muffled cries of those who are dying seem to vanish, as if a heavy curtain had fallen between that place where we once existed, because we suffered, and this other place where we now survive, but where we don't exist because we no longer dream. . . . And here we are again, amid the unending mechanized din of this life, in which — even though we may publicly deny it, and we do — we can't help but feel alien. The suit, the necktie, the briefcase, the car, the bills, the office, and above all, the ever-present wish for a trip south, far south. South as far as possible, to the very edge of horror.

· 38 ·

AS soon as Cleopatra saw the ambulance with the judo-trained emergency team, she realized that the doorman was being taken to an insane asylum, and immediately ordered the dove, the squirrel, and the rat to follow the vehicle. Here we should add that as soon as the doorman was not present, she abandoned human language and communicated with the rest of the animals by what we could call their traditional methods. Anyway, it was not difficult at all for us to guess the orders she had given. Those three animals not only followed the ambulance up to the psychiatric hospital — a huge gray building annexed to Bellevue Hospital — but they found out precisely (just as we did) which ward the patient was in, the treatment he was given, and the contacts he had there. Under Cleopatra's guidance, these animals visited the doorman almost every day, without his even knowing, and then they came back to Cleopatra with reports on the patient's condition.

The three animals, the dove, the squirrel, and even the rat, took special delight in clambering or flying to a cornice of the building or to a high branch where they could secretly watch the proceedings through the window. . . . We even have photos of the animals at work. But in spite of their excitement at being near the doorman, none of them spoke to him in any language. Apparently their job was solely to observe and then report what they saw to Cleopatra, without causing the doorman any more troubles than he already had, which were enough. We know the dog used to meet secretly with the three animals, so it would be fair to guess that the information she received is the same as what went into our own well-documented files.

The doorman's "magnetic ventriloquism" had been diagnosed by the most eminent psychiatrists as "the result of a strange case of chronic schizophrenia."

Committed to the hospital apparently on a permanent basis, our doorman managed, or tried, to communicate with some of the other psychiatric patients. We have obtained their medical case histories and their numbers. And we say *numbers* instead of *names* because, once admitted, patients are given code numbers stenciled on their uniforms. Our doorman was no longer Juan; he was now 23 666 017.

Among the patients Juan (or 23 666 017) got to know, we have 26 506, a lunatic whose mysterious derangement (for which the hospital doctors could not find a cure) made him obsessed with excrement. It was pathetic to see that poor man anxiously waiting for the time to take care of his physical functions so that he could immediately smear his whole body with excrement. Our doorman, during the moments that his daily doses of medication would allow, tried to convince him that this was not the solution or, in his words, not the "way out" of his problems. . . . Number 243 722 was a young, good-looking black man who had a mania for constantly dropping his pants in public and exposing his backside. For reasons we have not been able to determine, our doorman became the target of this inmate's gluteal exhibitions: so, wherever 23 666 017 was, 243 722 would point his ass in that direction. . . . Number 33 038 was an old woman whose odd obsession was to slit her wrists; her arms were all scarred and almost always covered with bandages. Number 160 114 was an older man of about sixty, a Cuban who had left his country on the Mariel boat lift of 1980, like our doorman. From the boat he had gone almost directly to the hospital because he refused to eat. He was being force-fed artificially by several nurses every day and only thanks to this had he survived. The strange thing about this case was that he would go to the dining hall like everybody else, take the food he was handed, and then store it in a plastic bag under his bed. He would accumulate an arsenal of different kinds of food but never even taste them, and the hospital employees had to come and throw everything into the garbage. When this happened, and it did pretty often, 160 114 went beserk and had to be restrained with a straitjacket. Juan sometimes would also save his food in a plastic bag and give it to his countryman, who, watching him suspiciously, would put it under his bed without saying a word.

Another inmate Juan tried to befriend was number 40 001, a lady about fifty-five, whose fixation was to introduce into her vagina every solid object she could find, even the knives and forks that kept disappearing from the dining hall. And there was also madman 322 289, "the professor," who earnestly told our doorman that the whole asylum was but a ship that had run aground due to technical difficulties, and that one of these days, through the research he was conducting, he would be able to get it running again. And when the boat finally set sail, he assured Juan, all of their problems would be over. Occasionally Juan would join his cause and help him convert hospital bed sheets into long strips, essential, according to the madman, for the salvage operation. Juan surely did not believe a word of this, but would go along with it for the chance to interpolate into the wacky professor's long scientific perorations a phrase or two he thought might offer some guidance. . . .

Inmates 20 190 and 25 177 were a pair of true exhibitionists. Not a day went by without their attempts to gain attention in the most unexpected ways: from walking on their hands to cutting off an ear, from streaking naked through the visiting room to trying to set themselves on fire at bathing time. They were two young men, short, baldish, and a bit overweight, with such unexciting bodies that nobody would give them a second look. Often they had to be gagged at night because they made strange noises, demanding to be heard, and kept all the other patients awake. There was another inmate whose syndrome manifested itself in a similar way. It was number 19 681, whom the nurses called "the preacher." He was about forty-five, and besides being adamant in refusing to bathe, he would go into tiresome and incoherent sermons based on some random word he had heard. No matter what word it was, be it a noun or verb or whatever, that man would always manage to build an interminable and impassioned thesis around it. When he finished, many of the other inmates and even some of the nurses would applaud him. It was very difficult for the doctors to use any therapy on this patient: the moment they said "Good morning," he would jump into a long dissertation on the word "morning," complete with quotations in Latin and French. He would at times be strangely lucid, even brilliant; but then he would get lost in the most bizarre conjectures, which on occasion would end in a sort of groan or whinny. . . .

And what could we say about 23 700 407, one of the newest patients — a Cuban, by the way — who kept on repeating the word *cacarajícara*? A word for which there is no English equivalent, and which maybe does not mean anything in particular, but it has a charming sound. Who knows what mysterious meaning or meanings this word had for him? Sometimes — actually six times, according to our records — Juan would approach this young man, who was about his age, and by way of greeting would say to him, "*Cacarajícara.*"

"*Cacarajícara?*" inmate 23 700 407 would then ask in astonishment. "*Cacarajícara,*" our doorman would confirm, trying to sound as friendly as possible, to see if they could establish some contact. "*Cacarajícara!!*" 23 700 407 would scream and, terrified, would seek refuge in a corner and repeat in a low, remotely tender voice, the word *cacarajícara* in every humanly possible inflection.

The maternal madwoman (all asylums have at least one) was 869 981, a woman about sixty with disheveled hair, who was always embracing a Raggedy Ann doll no one could wrest from her arms. What puzzled the psychiatrists was that this woman was the mother of twelve children whom she did not want to see when they came to visit her, preferring to stay in bed talking to her doll.

In most of these cases the derangement manifested itself in some form of "chattiness," but there were other patients who were absolutely withdrawn. One of them, 399 112, had never, as far as anybody knew, said a single word. Silence seemed to be his obsession, to such an extent that when someone spoke, the poor man covered his ears with his hands and his face contorted as if in great pain. One day the doorman found him almost suffocated in his bed. In order not to hear the sermons from 23 700 407, he had put his head under a dozen pillows and, on top of those, had managed to throw several of the very thin hospital mattresses. On this bouncy platform, numbers 20 190 and 25 177 were performing a naked dance while the young Cuban shouted mournfully, "*Cacarajícara! Cacarajícara!*"

The last inmate our doorman tried to make friends with was known as "the Cross Man," that is, 281 033. He was a gaunt man of uncertain age, with a sharp, chiseled face, who sometimes left a trail of blood behind him. On several occasions he had tried to crucify himself, and once actually succeeded. The administration of the hospital never found out how he did it (we happen to know he got some help from a nurse called James), but 281 033 got hold of two good pieces of wood, a hammer, and some nails, and one morning he was found actually crucified. An investigation was carried out among patients and employees, but no traces were found on the wood or on his body, other than those of the crucified man himself. Number 281 033 had made the cross alone. Before nailing it to the wall, he had had the foresight to hammer a large, sharp nail from the back of the right arm of the cross, so that the point came out through the other side. He nailed his two feet and one hand to the cross, and then swung the other hand back with tremendous force so that the protruding nail would go through it. Our doorman was the first one to see him on the cross. He was moaning softly, his body covered only by a hospital towel around his waist, and there was blood running down his legs onto the base of the wooden cross. The doorman called the nurses on duty, who took some time to come because it was well past midnight. While he waited, Juan removed the towel from the crucified man to wipe his wounds. And then he discovered that the man was not really a man: between his legs there was the bleeding sexual organ of a woman. Apparently he was an unfortunate transsexual, the victim of a botched sex-change operation that had left him with a defective orifice. The most surprising thing for the doorman (and for us too) was that the patient had shown no signs whatever of effeminacy, and did not even seem interested in anything sexual. But the doorman understood then the reason for the bloodstains that trailed behind the patient wherever he went.

Even though our doorman tried to communicate one way or the other with all these people, they paid very little attention, if any, to whatever he said. The explanation is simple: madness is perhaps the only state in which human beings apparently need no advice at all.

Evidently Juan's frustrated attempts to relate to these human beings, the sessions of acoustic therapy he was subjected to, and the multitude of pills he had to take were, over time, putting him in an almost deathly stupor; he would walk dragging his feet, sleep twelve or fifteen hours a day, and let days and weeks go by without saying a word. Even writing his notes, which he had kept doing secretly, became less and less frequent until he stopped altogether. He had gained considerable weight, and his attractive, swarthy complexion became milky-whitish and transparent, perhaps due to his being locked up indoors all the time, as well as the kind of food he had to eat. Only one thing about him remained unchanged: the occasional gleam of intense sadness in his eyes. It didn't go unnoticed by a dove, a squirrel, and a rat who came around to the hospital every day.

B E F O R E continuing with the final events of our story, we should state, in honor of the truth, that we did try indirectly on several occasions to improve the conditions surrounding Juan while at the mental hospital. We sent him better food than what he was served there (though it wasn't really bad), some books, and personal items. Finally, when we found out that, since the patient did not seem to improve, the hospital administration had determined to send him to a facility for the hope-lessly insane (a sort of hospital-prison with cell blocks and strict regulations, north of New York State), we sent through a third party a sort of petition for "clinical clemency." Even one of the social workers in our community visited Juan. She told him point-blank what lay in store for him and warned him there was only one way to avoid it: to deny he had had any relationship at all with the animals and, above all, to insist that his mind had briefly gone blank or that he had suffered some kind of temporary insanity during the time that he was imitat-ing various animals and talking to them, but that all of that had passed and his mind was clear now.

"The truth is I didn't talk to them," Juan protested in ear-nest. "They invited me to listen to them."

Our social worker left the hospital totally discouraged. She was a reliable, good woman, who knew everything about the doorman and had come to respect him.

"The worst thing of all is that he is only telling the truth," concluded that fine woman.

"Of course he's only telling the truth," agreed our representa-tive, who was some kind of philosopher. "Isn't truth the crazi-est thing?"

We felt there was nothing else to do. With the social worker's last attempt, we closed our doorman's case history. To go be-yond this point would have meant to endanger our hard-earned reputation as a reliable and powerful community in this coun-try and in the world. It would have been extremely risky to present ourselves publicly as the defenders or champions of someone who says (as the records of the investigation show) that he has heard the voices of twelve different animals. Imag-ine the Mayor of Miami (a notable Cuban), or the one from Hialeah (another prominent Cuban), or the president of Coca-Cola (a Cuban, of course), or the chancellor of Florida Interna-tional University (Cuban too), or the chief editor of the Spanish edition of *The Miami Herald* (another Cuban), or the director of Editorial Playor (also Cuban), or many other personalities as respectable as all those mentioned. Could you picture any of these people signing a document attesting to the mental health, and calling for the discharge from the hospital, of a young man who insists he heard a housefly talk?

However, it wasn't he alone who heard her talk, we did too!

Yes, we had to let his case go, at least in its clinical aspect, but we have maintained our discreet surveillance of the doorman.

Therefore, though we had nothing to do with the mysterious escape of patient 23 666 017 from an eleventh-floor ward (with double-barred windows), which took place in the early hours of the morning of April 4, 1991, we do know how it all came about.

O U R doorman had fallen into the deep sleep produced by the increasingly large dosage of pills he was being given. When he finally awoke, the orangutan and the rattlesnake were pulling apart the bars at his window, while the rat, the squirrel, the mice, and even the baby mice, plus other members of the rodent family, were gnawing feverishly at the wall where the bars were set. Countless pigeons and doves were also pecking at the windowpanes. Brenda Hill's cat meowed from the top of a tree in order to drown out the noise the other animals were making at the window. Below, hidden in the bushes of the hospital garden, Cleopatra, along with the bear, watched the maneuvers.

The bars finally gave way and fell to the lawn. The parrots pecked at the window panes until they broke. They were the first to get into the doorman's room, quickly followed by the ape and the snake. In a flash, the orangutan lifted Juan, placed him on his chest as he would do with his own baby orang, and asked him to hang on. As a safety precaution, the snake curled around them, locking the two ends of her body in a strong knot. Followed by the birds and the rodents, the ape sprang down from window to window until they reached the spot where Cleopatra was waiting. The cat stopped meowing and they all returned, as fast as they could, to the basement of their own building. Waiting for them there, or behind the bushes in the inner courtyard, were all the other animals, including the fly and even the golden fish in their bowl, which the ape had been wise enough to hide. In a whisper, Cleopatra quickly told the doorman everything the squirrel, the dove, and the rat had reported, particularly about the maximum-security hospital for the incurably insane where he was scheduled to be sent. In view of this, all the animals, including the dog, the cat, and the rabbit, had decided that the only option was to escape. "Because," Cleopatra now raised her voice, speaking to the doorman but also for the benefit of the other animals, "if they locked you up for life just for being human and talking to the animals, what would happen to us if one day they discovered that we, the animals, talk to you (and shall continue to do so)? At the very least they would lock us up for good, too!"

"Or what is worse," quickly added the Oscars' bulldog, "they would exhibit us in the circus for the rest of our lives, where on top of having to talk all the time, we could only say what they wanted."

"Working in a circus would not be anything new to you," sneered Brenda Hill's cat.

"I don't want to spend my life in a circus riding a tricycle or playing with a ball," moaned the bear.

"No one can train me to dance in the circus," the cat insisted, "they never have, and they never will! Bears and dogs, yes, we see them dance in every circus. But a cat? Have you ever seen a dancing cat?"

"The fact is," said Cleopatra, cutting the discussion short, "at this moment we know what we want most of all, though later we may have different ideas: what we want is to escape from here. We won't be able to do anything as long as we stay close to humans, who, besides using us, either do not know what they want, or want what they don't know. Here is the great difference between people and animals. . . . They already have Bach, but then they want to listen to something else, and so they spend their lives changing from one noise to another, without listening to any music at all. I know this is just an example. You may or may not like Bach; and yet, animals don't have that endless thirst for novelty. But do you think that even the wisest people, who are sure they know exactly what they want, are satisfied when their wishes are fulfilled? These so-called prophets or philosophers, whose works are collected even by some people in this building, have only made clear that they know nothing, and they go on disgracefully contradicting themselves. In this way they manage to make themselves so desperate that some have made desperation their philosophy. Others aim to find satisfaction in abstinence, joy in sorrow, not to mention those who, in the name of peace, are constantly destroying each other. The saddest fact is that the world is saturated with the objects they have produced: whining, pretentious volumes, loaded with obscure phrases, nothing but gibberish from hysterical exhibitionists trying to prove what geniuses they are."

Here Cleopatra glanced at the doorman, who immediately recalled the day she fiercely destroyed a book he was reading. She had touched a point obviously close to her heart: "How can someone be wise who isn't even moderately happy? How can people be superior creatures when they don't really know who they are or what they want, things other creatures do know? Therefore, since we do know what we want, what we have to do is work for it. Besides escape, each of you wants something different for yourself, or at least not exactly the same as somebody else. Is it possible, then, to find a place where we can all live in harmony? I doubt it. But if we go west, we'll be by the sea, and if we go southward down the coast, someday we'll find a big mountain. At its base, in the sea, the fish can swim; the dove and all the other birds will be peaceful in the trees; there will surely be some stream, lake, or lagoon for the turtle, warm rocks for the snake, dirt for those who want to burrow, high places for those who like to howl or meow or jump as much as they please, and on the mountain there will be enough snow for the bear to build his home."

"I don't want to build any home," protested the bear, "I already said I only want a cave, a big hole."

"And I want a hole too, but a small hole," stammered the rabbit.

"We're not going to waste precious time now over the size of a hole," added the rat wisely, seeing it was almost dawn. "Once we reach that mountain, we'll dig all the holes we want."

"And just where is that mountain?" inquired the fly out of sheer curiosity, since she knew very well she would not live long enough to get there.

"I do not know," was Cleopatra's reply.

"Well, we have to get going, we have to start looking for it right now," said the orangutan.

· 40 ·

TWO days after starting out, the group stopped just outside Baltimore. There the dove asked Cleopatra if it was possible to stop by Washington, D.C., where several of her sisters were held prisoner at the home of José Gómez Sicre. Cleopatra answered that it was not on their itinerary, but that her sense of smell was telling her they ought to stop in that city. "Besides," she consoled the dove, "the whole world will soon know about our escape, and animals everywhere will follow our example. . . ."

Six more days of flying, sliding, hopping, and all, and they reached Cincinnati. Another week of journeying, and they were in St. Louis, where spring was in full bloom. Needless to say, the orangutan and the bear and even the birds helped carry the slower animals. Hundreds of doves and pigeons would get together and lift the lizards and the snakes into the air; the parrots, joined by many others along the way, grasped the fishbowl and the turtles in their talons, and they all flew together over the highest mountains. Of course, the dove did not waste such a good opportunity to try to convince the turtle that the air is the ideal element for any kind of living thing. But the turtle, who did not want to hear anything about heights, closed his eyes and pretended not to hear, just desperately hoping to touch solid ground again, and consoling himself by thinking that the fish, still swimming through the clouds in their fishbowl, must be having an even more difficult time. . . . Interestingly enough, a Wichita newspaper reported (May 17, 1991) that near Topeka some farmers claimed they had seen a fish-bowl flying over their stone houses. People thought the whole thing was too bizarre. In Tulsa, a woman declared she had seen a snake crossing the skies at full speed, but nobody took this seriously either, not even the Indians whose distant Aztec cousins had once worshipped a plumed serpent as their god. . . . .

When they arrived at Oklahoma City, the fly announced without a trace of sentimentality that it was time for her to die. "I must make clear," she stated very calmly, now without having to fly within the bear's breath to keep warm (it was the bear's turn then to suffer the inclemencies of the warm weather), "I must make clear," she repeated, "that my impending death is not due to any inconveniences caused by our trip; it's just that my time has come. I've lived for several months, which is unusual for a fly. We only live for weeks and, some-times, only for days. I owe my long life to the great adventure I have shared with you. Now I only would like you to grant me one last wish. I'll fly as high as I can, and then a bird should swoop down and eat me. That's what tradition demands!" she added with a commanding edge in her voice, seeing that some animals were beginning to protest. To urge them into action, she continued:

"Don't you realize that if someone in our group eats me, I will go on being with you? And if it's a bird, I'll be still fly-ing. . . ."

And without further ado, the fly soared against the evening light with a deep buzz. When she reached about five hundred feet, she stopped buzzing and began to descend. Immediately, doves, pigeons, parrots, and other birds flew up into the sky and maintained a solemn formation for a while before diving down. When they did, one of them undoubtedly ate the fly. By the time they landed it was dark already, so they perched here and there on the big mass of animals huddled together to rest. They closed their eyes and tucked their heads under their wings and went to sleep.

Since human beings have the distinctive habit of not going to bed until midnight, the doorman was still awake, walking around and observing the fantastic configuration of all those sleeping bodies. The bear, in the center, seemed to form a big belly; the ape, at the top, was curled in the shape of a huge, black head; the snake was sleeping stretched across the bear, looking like a pair of arms; and the chihuahuas, at the feet of the bear, seemed to extend his paws to make up the legs, with the two turtles like feet completing the monstrous figure. The doorman looked again and realized that the proportions were exactly those of a frightening, gigantic man.

Cleopatra had been resting against the trunk of a tree, but at this point she approached the doorman.

"Don't let it frighten you," she told Juan, pointing to the animals, "it's only a likeness."

And without another word, she returned to her tree, closed her eyes, and went back to sleep, standing as usual.

Two weeks later, the caravan was crossing the great basin of the Colorado River, where the snake, now in home territory, prepared for everyone's enjoyment a recital of Sioux Indian chants in her powerful, deep voice. The five chihuahuas, for old times' sake, couldn't help doing their sassy dancing to the music. . . . After this reprieve, they continued on their march, stopping only when absolutely necessary.

In this way, after forty-nine days of traveling, on the 23rd of June of 1991 they reached the shores of the Pacific Ocean. Juan was the one chosen to set the fish free in their own element. All the animals, including the rabbit, were jumping with joy around the doorman, who, with the fishbowl held up high, waded in until he was knee-deep in the water. With obvious emotion, he emptied the fishbowl into the ocean. The two golden fish quickly went under and, gathering force, leapt three times above the surface, happily splashing the doorman's face.

After the ceremony was over, Cleopatra stood in the sandy shore so the fish could also hear her, and announced her decision to withdraw from the group. The unexpected news shocked the animals. The rabbit let out a brief shriek and fainted, and the turtles had to dunk him in the waves to help him regain consciousness, even more frightened than before.

Cleopatra's decision was final because, as she explained, they had already reached the sea, and she felt her presence was no longer necessary. Now they only had to keep walking, swimming, or flying along the coastline until they came to the mountain. "If I continue with you, we shall all be captured," she explained. "You don't need to think very long to realize that those who regard themselves as my masters have been looking for me, and if they find me, they will also find you. By myself, it will be easier for me to hide. And as for you," the regal dog said, addressing the perplexed doorman, "you already know that the right place for you is with them. Try to learn their languages, which are much more beautiful, universal, and eternal than those of humans. It will be easy for you to learn them, and I have already seen you practicing, maybe unconsciously. Once you have completed this apprenticeship with animals, you will be ready to familiarize yourself with the languages of trees and plants, and those of rocks and other objects. This is very important, for one day you shall be the intermediary between them and human beings. And you should know," and here the dog lowered her voice as if she did not wish the rest of the group to hear what she was going to say, "even the most insignificant objects, or *things*, as humans call them, are constantly transcending their supposed limitations as 'things.' When you were living in the city, didn't you notice how suddenly, almost before your eyes, things would disappear — the scissors, the matches, your keys, your toothbrush, a bottle of aspirin, anything? And then you would find them in the most unexpected places, or right there under your nose! Listen to me, you did not actually misplace them: they traveled. This has been going on forever, but human beings cannot perceive it. . . . Things are trapped, just as we were. But when they find the slightest opportunity, they escape even if just for a moment. Drop something on the floor, a pill or a coin, and see how it runs into hiding behind the legs of the table or under the bed. Some day," Cleopatra went on, now raising her voice as if realizing that nothing had to be hidden from the rest of the group, "all things, all objects and machines, will claim their independence, either by natural right or by an awakening in some forgotten corner of their apparent inertia. Then, those so-called inanimate objects will go against the laws of nature created by humans, and assume their own, which are those of liberty and therefore of rebellion. It will be a total revolution. Stones will jump from their places and crack the skulls of pedestrians, forks will turn and poke out the eyes of people eating, necklaces will strangle ladies during their social receptions, toothpicks will pierce their users' tongues, and at the same time staircases will recoil and allow no one to climb them. Who could prevent the self-incineration of a suicidal library, the willful shattering of a crystal goblet, the voluntary unriveting of an aircraft fuselage, or the decision of an ocean liner to take passengers and crew to the bottom of the sea? . . . To awaken the latent instincts of all things will be your task, yours especially," proclaimed Cleopatra, looking the doorman in the eye, "but first you must find a place where you will not be disturbed. . . . And now I must leave."

"I believe," observed the rabbit timidly, "there might be a way for you to go unnoticed among us, and even among humans. Just dye your coat a different color. Look at me, I have even crossed the desert in my lavender coat and no rabbit ever approached me to say hello, and no wolf ever chased me, as they should by their nature."

"That doesn't mean they didn't recognize you. Anyone would be ashamed to talk to or even to eat a creature of that color, which, lucky for you, is beginning to fade away," commented the rat with her usual sarcasm.

"For camouflage I don't think you should dye your coat violet," volunteered the bear respectfully, speaking to Cleopatra, "but white, my natural color, which I'll soon have back again. White, I tell you, is a noble color that commands respect."

"Respect? Don't make me laugh!" snapped the parrot. "There are thousands of people around wearing white fur coats from all sorts of animals, including bears. Besides, white is a very dirty color where any spot stands out right away. The only disguise for Cleopatra is a suit made of feathers; yes, many feathers of different colors so she can blend with her surroundings. And I am quite willing to sacrifice some of mine."

"Enough!" the dog said. "I shall find my own way without having to give up my natural color."

"The trouble is she wants to go back to the city to listen to Bach," scowled the cat.

"Perhaps," Cleopatra replied. And she glanced over the whole group with her large violet, enigmatic eyes. . . . Then, turning away from the shore, she went with a light gait into the nearby woods. And though it was her natural pace, the doorman seemed to sense in it a feeling of sadness.

"She won't be able to survive by herself," commented one of the five chihuahuas, jumping all around Juan. "She is too aristocratic."

"What do you know about these things!" rebutted the squirrel. "I'm aristocratic too and I have been leaping across a whole continent."

"Ha! Just listen to her! Aristocratic!" cried the cat. "Look here, honey, it seems you have forgotten you are nothing but a rodent."

"And what's wrong with that?" the rat protested in defense of the squirrel, obviously offended by the cat's comment.

In between exchanges of this kind, the caravan continued, guided by the hypersensibility of the rattlesnake and the advice of the turtle, who would sometimes swim out in order to bring back scouting reports from the golden fish on the high seas. By the following day they were already in San Diego.

We don't know if it was due to mysterious and powerful instructions from Cleopatra or to some new migratory instinct awakened by the group, but as they advanced, they were joined by a great following of birds, animals, and all kinds of creatures.

Out of the nearby woods came wild dogs, boas, she-foxes with their new pups, deer, ferrets, llamas, mountain lions, skunks, tritons, and bison. From the plains in a thunderous rumble stampeded hundreds of buffalo. From the swamps came armies of frogs, crabs, alligators, otters, swans, and toads; from the *pedregal* emerged lizards, scorpions, iguanas, echerris, salamanders, quail, centipedes, phylloxera, and fleas. The sky was a single cloud of birds and flying insects, and the sea was thick with shoals of albacore, seals, sharks, schools of sardines, sea urchins, dolphins, sturgeon, and a thousand more aquatic creatures. Swimming among them, the two golden fish, still under the influence of their former owner, Mr. Lockpez, kept touching with their lips either the tail of a seahorse, or the whiskers of a porpoise, or the gills of a hybrid lambrus. . . . Descending from the trees were elegant coleoptera, tarantulas, caterpillars, small tree snakes, blue flies, crickets, bats, locusts, praying mantises, snails, and killjoys. Farther on they were joined by a flock of strange creatures: they had three legs but used only two, leaving the third one at rest; one of their eyes was on their forehead and the other one on the tail, and sometimes they moved forward making great circles. They said their generic name was "bobadilla,"* and they happily joined the caravan. . . . Cockroaches, cinenes, vultures, larks, eagles, sparrows, gnats, pelicans, butterflies, owls, wild and domestic hens, flamingos, sea gulls, hummingbirds, cuckoos, albatrosses, and mosquitoes joined the aerial procession. Cotingas, sheep, onagers, hornbills, wild boars, otarias, worms, mallards, petrels, and curlews also followed. A little farther ahead, preceded by their unanimous howling, came packs of wolves, and soon after, the cormorants. In a mountain pass a herd of cattle awaited them placidly. Across a vast prairie came the horses at full gallop.

I T was quite impressive to observe from a distance, as most of us did with the help of an excellent telescope, the steadily increasing stampede, though occasionally (it couldn't be otherwise!) one animal ate another. The group advanced with machinelike precision. The slower ones used the others as

---

* We wish to point out that not even one of the members of our powerful community who, disguised as various animals, had joined the exodus and were observing every detail, ever figured out what kind of animals these were. We suspect that they might be a long-forgotten invention of the deceased Mr. Skirius.

vehicles. Snails attached themselves like barnacles to the shells of turtles, and when the turtles discovered they were lagging behind, they would dive into the water and hitch a long ride on top of a large fish. Exhausted larks perched on alligators; chatty parrots rode spirited steeds. Even the doorman, who could already communicate with the animals in their own language, would sometimes ride an alpaca, a wild dog, or even a foul-smelling weasel.

When they reached the equator, the thunderous stampede was deafening.

· Conclusions ·

WE said at the beginning that we had decided to write the story of the doorman because something extraordinary had happened to him. Now, at the end of this report, we can positively state that Juan is quite mysterious and terrifying and that, since we are the only ones who know about him and know where he is, he also belongs to us. With his help we could equip the most heterogeneous and efficient army ever conceived by man.

We hope that this document (all forty chapters, to be exact), intelligently used, could serve as a warning for those who do not respect our exile community, or for those who have refused to take us seriously. Better be forewarned: *At present we are the sole possessors of a secret lethal weapon.*

Of course, the threat hangs over us and over all humanity, that these animals, gathered around the doorman, could decide to invade us, not to mention the horrifying theory that inanimate objects too could gain autonomy and destroy us. This also means that the possibility (or the responsibility?) to prevent this from happening rests on us. But we won't prevent it. A people forced out of their country and persecuted, a people in exile and who consequently suffer humiliation and discrimination, live for their day of revenge.

When that day comes, we'll need a much more powerful weapon than all the evil of our enemy, a weapon absolutely unknown to our so-called allies — so called because, thinking first and always of their personal safety, they will end up making pacts with the enemy.

Our only hope — our great weapon — is our doorman.

· The Door ·

A T the end there would be a door for the dove to enter into the land of her dreams, where she could feel at home right away. A huge door of green branches and creeping vines in perpetual bloom would await the parrot, the squirrel, the cat, and the orangutan, so they could keep playing forever. . . . A door made of warm rocks, a labyrinth of nooks and crannies, would open for the snake and the rat. An underground door, safe and therefore undetectable, for the rabbit. And a big door, broad and comfortable, in snow country, for the bear. A door composed of water and earth, immense and silent, for the turtle. And a door that would open into the vastness of the oceans for the fish. And beyond that one, a glittering door would be awaiting the fly, who, buzzing happily, would disappear among the gleams of light. . . . Yes, doors of sunshine, doors of water, doors of earth, doors of flowering vines, doors of ice, hanging doors or underground doors, tiny doors or immeasurable ones, deeper than the ocean, more transparent than the air, more luminous than the sky, would be awaiting the animals to take them to a place where nobody could spy on them through telescopes, or send undercover agents after us. . . . And through those doors everyone, finally, will eagerly rush in.

That is, all except me, the doorman, who on the outside will watch them disappear forever.

LOST DOG

REWARD
RARE EGYPTIAN BREED
ONLY ONE OF ITS KIND
BLACK COAT   LONG LEGS
LARGE VIOLET EYES
ANSWERS TO THE NAME OF 'CLEOPATRA'

$5,000 REWARD
PLEASE RETURN TO THE ADDRESS LISTED BELOW*

---

* This advertisement has appeared every day in *The New York Pet* since April 1991 to the present. Apparently, no one has been able to find Cleopatra.

The original manuscript for the novel *El portero*, written in New York City between April 1984 and December 1986, is part of the manuscript collection of Reinaldo Arenas deposited at the Princeton University Library, New Jersey.